the Vampire
Diaries

STEFAN'S DIARIES
VOL. 4   THE RIPPER

The Vampire Diaries novels

VOL. I: THE AWAKENING
VOL. II: THE STRUGGLE
VOL. III: THE FURY
VOL. IV: DARK REUNION
THE RETURN VOL. 1: NIGHTFALL
THE RETURN VOL. 2: SHADOW SOULS
THE RETURN VOL. 3: MIDNIGHT
THE HUNTERS VOL. 1: PHANTOM

Stefan's Diaries novels

VOL. I: ORIGINS
VOL. 2: BLOODLUST
VOL. 3: THE CRAVING
VOL. 4: THE RIPPER

The Secret Circle novels

THE INITIATION AND THE CAPTIVE PART I
THE CAPTIVE PART II AND THE POWER

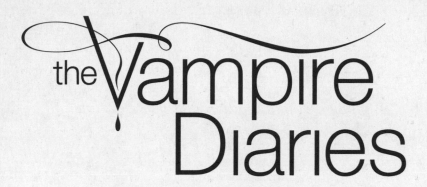

the Vampire Diaries

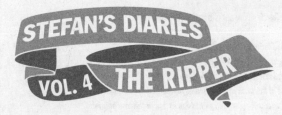

STEFAN'S DIARIES
VOL. 4   THE RIPPER

Based on the novels by
L. J. SMITH

and the TV series developed by
**KEVIN
WILLIAMSON
& JULIE PLEC**

HARPER TEEN
An Imprint of HarperCollinsPublishers

HarperTeen is an imprint of HarperCollins Publishers.

Stefan's Diaries Vol. 4: The Ripper

alloyentertainment
Produced by Alloy Entertainment
151 West 26th Street, New York, NY 10001
www.alloyentertainment.com

Library of Congress Cataloging-in-Publication Data is available.
ISBN 978-0-06-211393-1

Typography by Liz Dresner
11   12   13   14   15   CG/BV   10   9   8   7   6   5   4   3   2   1
❖
First Edition

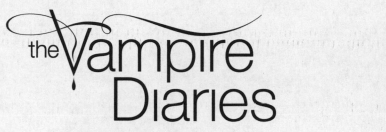

the Vampire Diaries

STEFAN'S DIARIES
VOL. 4 THE RIPPER

August 1888

How much can change in a year.

It's one of those phrases that I've caught in conversation, one that rattles in my mind like a pebble along a road, a vestige of my previous life. Once upon a time, a year was weighty, substantial. It was filled with possibilities: of meeting the love of your life, of having children, of dying. It was a stepping-stone on the path of life—a path that I no longer walk.

A year was one thing. Twenty years ago, when my entire world turned upside down, was something else entirely.

A year ago, I came to England, a land so

steeped in history it makes the prospect of eternity seem less overwhelming. And although the setting had changed, I stayed the same. I still looked like I had the day I turned into a vampire, and the same thoughts—of Katherine, who turned me, of Damon, my brother, of the death and destruction that I could never, ever seem to erase—still haunted my dreams. Time had been steadily galloping forward, but I remained as before, a demon desperate for redemption.

If I were a human, I'd be comfortably in middle age by now. I'd have a wife, children, perhaps even a son I'd prepare to take over my family business.

Before the Salvatore family business became murder.

It's a legacy I've spent the past twenty years trying to correct, hoping that somehow an eternity of good deeds could make up for the mistakes I have made, the blood I have shed.

And in some ways, it has; England was good for me. Now, I'm an honest man—or as honest as a man can be when his past is as wretched as mine.

I no longer feel guilty for draining the blood of woodland creatures. I am, after all, a vampire. But I am not a monster. Not anymore.

Still, time does not touch me as it does humans, nor does each new year turn over with the breathless anticipation of those who live. All I can hope is that each year will carry me further and further from the destruction of my youth with no fresh pain on my conscience. If I could have that, it would be my salvation.

unlight dappled the rough-hewn beams of the expansive kitchen of Abbott Manor, where I was employed as a groundskeeper. I sighed in contentment as I gazed out the thick windows at the verdant rolling countryside surrounding the home. Although meticulously kept up by Mrs. Duckworth, the Abbotts' devoted housekeeper, I could see motes of pollen floating through the bright rays. The homey, comfortable setting reminded me of the Veritas Estate, where pollen from the magnolia trees would drift through the open windows and coat an entire room in a thin layer of dust.

"Can you pass me the knife, Stefan?" Daisy, one of the young housemaids, asked as she flirtatiously batted her eyelashes at me. Daisy was a local girl occasionally employed by Mrs. Duckworth to come in and assist in the kitchen for the day. A short girl with curly brown hair and a smattering of freckles across her upturned nose, she reminded me of Amelia Hawke, one of my childhood friends from Mystic Falls. Amelia would now most likely have children Daisy's age, I realized.

"Why, of course, Daisy darlin'," I said in my exaggerated Southern accent, bowing deeply to her. Daisy always teased me about how American I sounded, and I enjoyed our lighthearted exchanges. They were playful and innocent, a reminder that words didn't always carry an ulterior motive.

I pulled a knife from a drawer and passed it to her as she plucked a cucumber from a large wooden bowl and set it down on the table, biting her lip in concentration.

"Ow!" Daisy yelped, yanking her finger away from the cucumber and hastily bringing her hand to her lips. She turned toward me, blood oozing from the wound.

I felt my fangs begin to bulge from underneath my gums. I gulped and stepped away, trying to stop the transformation while I still had the chance.

"Stefan, help!" Daisy implored.

I staggered back as the scent of blood invaded my nostrils and seeped into my brain. I could imagine how sweet the liquid would taste on my tongue.

I grabbed a napkin and thrust it toward her. I squeezed

my eyes shut, but if anything, it only made the metallic scent of blood more potent.

"Here!" I said roughly, blindly shaking the napkin at her. But she did not take it, so I opened one eye, then the other. Daisy was standing there, her arm outstretched, but something about her was different. I blinked again. It wasn't my imagination. Her mousy brown hair had transformed into a shiny red copper, while her full cheeks had slimmed into an angular face that had only the faintest dusting of freckles across the bridge of her nose.

Somehow, Daisy had disappeared, and a new figure stood in her place.

"Callie?" I croaked, steadying myself against the wooden table. Callie Gallagher—fiery, impetuous, fiercely loyal, and dead by Damon's hand—was right in front of me. My mind was whirling. What if she hadn't really died? Could she somehow have escaped to England to start over? I knew it didn't make sense, but she was right in front of me, as lovely as ever.

"Stefan . . ." she whispered, tilting her face toward me.

"Callie!" I smiled as my fangs receded. I felt a quickening in my chest, a shadow of the human emotions that Callie had helped me remember. I reached out toward her, brushing my hand against her shoulder, allowing my nose to inhale her apple-and-hay scent. But as soon as I blinked again, to take her all in, everything about her changed. Her lips were parted too widely, her teeth too white, her eyes bloodshot. A lemon-and-ginger fragrance wafted through the air.

I blinked in horror. Fear ran through my veins like ice. Could it be . . .

It was Katherine. *Katherine*. The first woman I ever believed myself to fall in love with. The vampire who stole my heart only as a means to steal my soul. "Leave me be!" I called raggedly, scrambling backward so quickly my foot caught on the table leg. I steadied myself. I knew I had to get away from her. She was evil. She'd destroyed me. And yet, she looked so lovely. A mischievous expression danced across her face.

"Why, hello, Stefan," she said in a dulcet tone as she advanced toward me. "Did I scare you? You look as if you've seen a ghost!"

"You're dead," I spat, still unable to believe she was in front of me.

She laughed, a sound as warm and enveloping as whiskey on a cold winter night.

"Wasn't I always? It's good to see you. You look well. Although maybe a bit too pale," Katherine admonished.

"How did you get here?" I asked finally. Her body had been burned, buried in a Virginia church an ocean away. And yet, it was undeniable that she was standing not two feet from me in the Abbott kitchen.

"I needed to see you," Katherine said, biting her lower

lip with her perfectly white teeth. "I'm terribly sorry, Stefan. I feel we had so many misunderstandings. I never truly explained myself or my nature to you. Do you think you could ever forgive me?" she asked.

I found myself nodding, despite my hatred for what she'd done to me. I knew I needed to flee, but I couldn't look away from Katherine's large eyes. I wasn't being compelled. It was worse. I was being driven by love. I tentatively reached out and allowed my fingers to graze her skin. It was smooth, and instantly I was consumed with the need to touch her again and again.

"Sweet Stefan," Katherine cooed, as she leaned toward me. Her petal-soft lips brushed against my cheek. I leaned in, succumbing to her lemon-ginger scent. My desire, suppressed for twenty years, was unleashed. I didn't care about the past. I didn't care what she'd done to me or my brother. I wanted her. My lips hungrily found hers, and I kissed her, sighing with happiness and contentment.

She pulled back, and my gaze lifted to her face. Her eyes were bulging, and her fangs were glinting in the sunlight.

"Katherine!" I gasped. But I couldn't escape. Her icy-cold hands were around my neck, drawing me into her, and then I felt a searing pain at my throat. I tried to turn away but the pain went deeper, farther into my body until it reached into the depths of my soul. . . .

Everything around me went dark.

And then I heard a sharp, persistent knocking.

"Katherine?" I groped around in confusion as I realized I was bathed in sweat. I blinked. Above me was the sloped roof of my thatched cottage. Sunlight streamed in through the cracks in the ceiling.

The knocking continued.

I scrambled from my bed and pulled on my breeches and shirt. "Come in!" I called.

The door swung open and Mrs. Duckworth bustled in, concern stamped on her round, red face. "You all right, then?" Mrs. Duckworth asked.

"Fine. Just a dream," I said, shifting uneasily from one foot to another. *Was* it just a dream? I hadn't thought about her in ages, but in my dream, Katherine had seemed so real, so *alive.*

"Having a nightmare, you was," Mrs. Duckworth said knowledgeably, crossing her arms across her expansive, matronly chest. "I could hear you yelling outside the door. And you gave me a right fright, I'd thought you were attacked by one of them foxes from the woods. Mrs. Medlock up at the Evans farm said one got a few of their chickens the other day. In broad daylight, too!"

"A nightmare . . ." I repeated, as I steadied myself against the wooden post of my bed. The sun was just beginning its descent and the forest outside my window was blanketed in an amber light.

"Yes," Mrs. Duckworth replied patiently. She was wearing a starched white apron over her blue-and-white-striped dress, and her gray hair was pulled back in a severe bun. She'd been a servant at the Manor for over twenty years, and oversaw everything that went on in the house with a motherly concern. George Abbott always joked that she, not him, was truly in charge. Seeing her calmed me, a reminder that the events were all in my head, and that I was safe here. "I just hope the missus didn't hear you. Wouldn't want her to think you was haunted."

"Not me," I said impatiently, picking up my bedclothes and tossing them back on the bed. I didn't like the implication of Mrs. Duckworth's colloquialisms, or that she was never quite able to produce a grammatically correct sentence. "You mean *the cabin* is haunted. Which it's not," I said quickly.

"No, I meant you's haunted," Mrs. Duckworth said sagely. "You must have something in your mind that's troubling you. Not letting you rest."

I looked down at the rough, uneven floorboards. It was true. Even though I had fled from home, I was still haunted by visions from my past. Sometimes, when I dreamt of Damon and myself as children, racing horses against each other through the Virginia woods, the dreamscapes were pleasant. Other times, they reminded me that even though I was destined to live on Earth for eternity, a part of me was always in hell.

"No matter," Mrs. Duckworth said, crisply brushing her hands together to create a loud clapping sound. "I was coming to fetch you for Sunday supper. The boys can't stop asking for you," she said, an affectionate smile on her face as she spoke of Luke and Oliver, the two young Abbott boys.

"Of course," I said. I loved Sunday suppers. They were casual and noisy, filled with delicious food and good-natured bickering between Luke and Oliver. Their father, George, would bounce four-year-old Emma, the youngest Abbott, on his knee, while their mother, Gertrude, would smile proudly at her brood. I'd sit at the far edge of the table, thankful that I, too, was part of the tableaux. They were just a normal family, enjoying a typical Sunday. And to me, there was nothing—not the finest mansions in San Francisco or the glittering, champagne-soaked balls of New York City—that could possibly compare.

When I'd come to Abbott Manor last fall, I had only the shirt on my back and a horse I'd won in a game of cards at a portside bar just outside of Southampton. She'd been a black beauty who'd reminded me of Mezzanotte, my horse from my Virginia childhood. I'd named her Segreto, Italian for *secret*, and we spent the month roaming the countryside before arriving in Ivinghoe, a town about fifty miles outside of London. Looking for someone who would purchase Segreto, I'd been directed to George Abbott, who, upon

hearing my carefully crafted tale of woe, had offered me
both the price of the horse and a job as caretaker.

"You best hurry up," Mrs. Duckworth said, interrupt-
ing my memory. She strode out of my cottage, closing the
door with a thud.

I glanced hastily at my reflection in the looking glass
that hung over my simple chest of drawers. I quickly
slicked my brown hair back and ran my tongue over my
gums. My fangs rarely made an appearance anymore, at
least not in my waking hours. I'd even taken to hunting my
prey with a bow and arrow, then draining the blood into
a glass and drinking it as I relaxed by the fire. I remember how my friend Lexi had tried and tried to get me to
take goat's blood tea, back when I was a young vampire,
wreaking havoc on the city of New Orleans. Back then, I'd
resisted, thinking goat's blood was an affront to what blood
should taste like—rich, sweet, human.

If only she could see me now, I thought ruefully. I sometimes wished that she was here, especially during the long,
dark nights. It would be nice to have someone to talk
to, and Lexi was a true friend. But she and I had parted
ways upon reaching Britain. She'd decided to go on to the
Continent, while I chose to stay and see what the country
had to offer. It was just as well. Although we'd parted on
good terms, I could sense sometimes she grew impatient
with my melancholic disposition. I didn't blame her. I grew

impatient with myself, too, wishing that I could simply move on. I wished I could flirt with Daisy without fear of my fangs making an appearance. I wished I could discuss my former life in America with George without letting slip that I'd been alive during the Civil War. And I wished, more than anything, I could erase Damon from my mind. I felt that being by myself and on my own two feet was what I needed to move forward. Until one nightmare would send me back into my misery.

But only if I let it. I'd learned that memories were just that—memories. They had no power to hurt me, unless I let them. I learned that I could trust humans. And late at night, my body warmed by badger blood and listening to the sounds of the forest come to life, I felt almost happy.

There was little excitement and adventure. What there was—and what I was thankful for—was routine. The job was much like what I'd been doing in my youth in Virginia, back when Father had been priming me to take over Veritas Estate. I bought livestock, oversaw the horses, and mended anything that might need fixing. I knew George approved of my work, and we were even going into London tomorrow to discuss the finances of the farm, a true sign of his trust in me. In fact, the entire Abbott family seemed to like me, and I was surprised to find how much I liked them. I knew in a few years I'd have to move on, since they'd soon notice that I wasn't aging as they were. But I could still enjoy the time I had left.

Hastily, I pulled on a merino-wool jacket, one of the many items of clothing George had given me in the few short months I'd been at Abbott Manor. Indeed, he often said he thought of me like a son, a sentiment which simultaneously warmed and amused me. If only he knew that he was actually a few years younger than me. He took his position as a father figure seriously, and although he could never replace my real father, I welcomed the gesture.

Not bothering to lock the door to my cottage, I strode up the hill to the house, whistling a nameless tune. Only as I got to the chorus did I realize its origin—it was "God Save the South," one of Damon's favorites.

Grimacing, I mashed my lips together and practically ran the remaining steps to the rear door of the manor. After twenty years, any recollection of Damon was as sharp and abrupt as a clap of thunder on a dry, hot summer day. I still remembered him—his brooding blue eyes, his lopsided smile, and his sarcasm-tinged Southern accent—as vividly as if I'd only seen him ten minutes ago. Who knew where he was now?

He could even be dead. The possibility sprang into my mind out of nowhere. I uneasily shook off the thought.

Arriving at the house, I swung open the door. The Abbotts never kept it locked. There was no need. The next house was five miles down the road, the town another two beyond that. Even then, the town only consisted of a pub, post office, and train station. There was nowhere safer in all of England.

"Stefan, my boy!" George called eagerly, striding into the foyer from the sitting room. Giddy and already a little drunk on pre-supper sherry, George was flushed and seemed even more rotund than last week.

"Hello, sir!" I said enthusiastically, glancing down at him. He stood at only a little bit above five feet, and his bulk seemed to be his way of making up for his short stature. Indeed, sometimes I worried for the horses when it struck George's fancy to go for a ride in the woods.

But even though the other servants occasionally mocked him for his unwieldy body and fondness for drink, I saw in him nothing but friendliness and goodwill. He'd taken me in when I had nothing, and not only had he given me a roof over my head, but he'd given me hope that I could find companionship with humans again.

"Spot of sherry?" George asked, pulling me out of my reverie.

"Of course," I said amiably, as I settled into one of the comfortable red velvet chairs in the sitting room, a small and homey space with Oriental rugs covered in dog hair. Gertrude Abbott had a soft spot for the farm dogs, and would let them inside the Manor whenever it rained—which was nearly every day. The walls were covered with portraits of Abbott relatives, identifiable by their dimples. That made all of them, even a stern portrait of Great-uncle Martin, who stood watch over the bar in the corner, seem almost friendly.

"Stefan!" A lisping voice shrieked as the two Abbott boys tumbled into the room. First came Luke, devious and dark-haired, with a cowlick that simply wouldn't behave no matter how much his mother pushed it down against his forehead. Oliver followed, a seven-year-old with straw-colored hair and skinned knees.

I smiled as Oliver threw his arms around my legs. A stray piece of hay from the barn was stuck in his hair, and his freckled face was smudged with dirt. He'd most likely been out in the woods for hours.

"I hunted a rabbit! He was this big!" Oliver said, breaking away and holding his hands several feet apart.

"That big?" I asked, raising my eyebrows. "Are you sure it was a rabbit? Or was it a bear?" Oliver's light eyes grew saucerlike at the possibility, and I stifled a smile.

"It *wasn't* a bear, Stefan!" Luke interjected. "It was a rabbit, and I was the one who shot it. Oliver's bullet only scared it."

"Did not!" Oliver said angrily.

"Daddy, tell Stefan! Tell him I shot it!"

"Now, boys!" George said, smiling fondly at his two

young sons. I grinned as well, despite the pang of regret I felt stabbing into the core of my being. It was such a familiar scene that I knew played out in houses all over the world: Sons squabbled, rebelled, and grew up, and then the cycle repeated all over again. Except in the case of me and my brother. As children, we'd been exactly like Oliver and Luke. We were rough-and-tumble and unafraid to knock each other down, because we knew that our fierce, undying loyalty would spur us to help each other back up moments later. Before Katherine had come between us and changed everything.

"I'm sure Stefan doesn't want to hear you boys bickering," George added, taking another swig of sherry.

"I don't mind," I said, ruffling Oliver's hair. "But I think I need to enlist you to help me with a problem. Mrs. Duckworth said there's a fox in the forest who's been stealing the chickens from the Evanses' coop, and I know that only the best hunter in all of England will be able to bring down the beast," I invented.

"Really?" Oliver asked, his eyes growing wide.

"Really." I nodded. "The only person who can possibly take him down is someone small and quick and very, very clever." I saw interest flicker across Luke's face. At nearly ten, he most likely felt too grown-up to take part, but I knew he wanted to. Damon had been similar at that age— too sophisticated to be caught enjoying the games that we'd all play down by the creek, yet terrified of missing out on anything.

"And maybe we'll take your brother," I said in a stage whisper, winking as I caught George's eye. "The three of us will be the best hunting party this side of London. The fox won't stand a chance."

"Sounds like a fine adventure!" George said grandly as his wife, Gertrude, walked in. Her red hair was pulled back, emphasizing the widow's peak on her fair forehead, and she was carrying their four-year-old daughter, Emma, on her hip. Emma had fine blond hair and enormous eyes, and often looked more like a fairy or a sprite than a human child. She flashed me a large grin and I smiled back, feeling happiness radiate from the center of my being.

"Will you come, Daddy?" Oliver asked. "I want you to see me hunt."

"Ah, you know me," George said, shaking his head. "I'd only scare the fox into the bushes. He'd hear me coming from a mile away," he said.

"Stefan could teach you to be quiet!" Oliver lisped.

"Stefan's already teaching this old man to run his farm," George laughed ruefully.

"Sounds to me like we're all telling stories tonight," I said good-naturedly. Even though the work was demanding, I truly enjoyed the time I spent on the farm with George. It was so different from how I'd felt at Veritas, working under my own father. Back then, I'd resented being kept on the farm, instead of being allowed to go to the University of Virginia. I'd hated feeling like my father was constantly judging and appraising me, wondering if I was worthy of taking over the estate. But with the Abbotts, I felt like I was appreciated for the man I was.

I took a deep sip of sherry and leaned back into the chair, shaking off the final unsettling images from my earlier nightmare. Katherine was dead. Damon might very well be, too. *This* was my reality now.

2

The next morning, George and I were settled in a lavish train car on our way to London. I leaned back in the plush chair, allowing waves of nausea to ride over me. I knew from past experiences that cities could be too loud, too heavy with the scent of unwashed bodies, too tempting. So in preparation, I'd drunk the blood of a skunk and a hare, and now felt sick. But better sick than starving, especially since I wanted to put my best foot forward when we met with George's solicitor. I knew it was an honor for him to invite me to meet his associate, a man who'd look over the numbers from the farm and advise us if there was anything we needed to do differently when it came to staffing and purchasing.

And yet, I simply couldn't shake the image of Katherine

from my nightmare. So instead of talking, I merely nodded as George wondered aloud whether or not we should
lease out our horses to the mine at the other side of
Ivinghoe. It was impossible to shift from life and death
to the minutiae of human existence. In another twenty
years—ten even—none of it would matter.

The velvet curtain of our compartment opened, and a
porter popped his head in.

"Tea or newspaper?" he asked, holding out a silver tray
piled high with scones and teacakes. Mr. Abbott eyed them
hungrily as the porter placed tea and two raisin scones on
pristine china plates and then passed one to each of us.

"You can have mine," I said, handing the plate over to
Mr. Abbott. "We'll take the newspaper as well."

"Right, sir." The porter nodded and passed me a copy
of the *Daily Telegraph*.

Immediately, I pulled out the pages I enjoyed, handing
George the features he loved while I kept the sports and
society pages for myself. It was an odd combination, but it
had been my habit for the past twenty years, whenever I
found myself in a city, to read the society news. I wanted
to look for any mention of Count DeSangue, the name that
Damon had used in New York. I wondered if he'd given up
his airs and grandiose posturing. I hoped so. The last time
I saw him, his showiness had nearly led to our demise. It
was far better for us both to go under the radar.

> *Bram Stoker and Henry Irving open new play*
> *at the Lyceum . . . Sir Charles Ainsley invites*
> *guests to his West End House . . . Samuel Mortimer*
> *rumored to be running for London Councillor . . .*
> *dashing Count DeSangue seen out on the town at*
> *the supper club the Journeyman with lovely lady*
> *of the stage Charlotte Dumont.*

I felt my stomach clench with recognition. It was exactly as I expected. Seeing the words was a clear sign that Damon was still haunting me; a sign I couldn't attribute to my dream, an overactive imagination, or too much sherry the night before. Because even though Damon hated me more than anything, it didn't change the fact that I was his brother. I'd known him my whole life. As children, I could sense that he'd have a fight with Father even before it happened. There would be tension crackling in the air, as evident as clouds before a storm. I could tell when he was angry, even if he was smiling at all our friends, and I always knew when he was frightened, even though he'd never, ever say it. Even as vampires, something deep within me was still connected to his moods. And whether he knew it or not, he was in trouble.

I scanned the rest of the column, but that was the only mention of Damon. The rest was about lords and dukes and earls, which must have been Damon's newest set. Not that I was surprised. London, with its endless parties and cosmopolitan atmosphere, had always struck me as a place Damon could end up. Human or demon, he'd always cut an impressive figure. And whether I liked it or not, he was my brother. The same blood ran through our veins. If I felt a pull toward England, wouldn't it make sense that he would, too?

I glanced down at the paper again.

Who was Charlotte Dumont? And where was the Journeyman? Maybe, if I had time in London after the solicitor's appointment, I'd head out on my own to find it. It would at least lay my uneasy feelings to rest. After all, I was sure he was drinking Charlotte Dumont's blood, but if that was the extent of Damon's misbehavior, who was I to say anything? And if he was doing something *worse*, well . . . I'd cross that bridge when I came to it.

Across from me, George was stabbing his knife into the pat of butter. What he had in wealth and land, he lacked in table manners. But instead of repulsing me, his boorish behavior yanked me out of my head. Our eyes caught, and I sensed George appraising my grass-stained blue shirt and black slacks. They were the nicest clothes I owned, but I knew they made me look like a laborer.

"I think while we're in town, I might take you to my tailor. Have some suits made," George mused.

"Thank you, sir," I mumbled. We were getting closer to

the city, and the scenery had changed from wide expanses of open land to clusters of low-roofed houses. "But I'd actually like to explore the city on my own after the meeting. You see, I have some relations in London. If it's all right with you, I'd like to take a few days to see them. I'll be sure to mend that fence at the far end of the pasture as soon as I return," I lied. I'd never asked for days off. If George showed an ounce of hesitation, then I wouldn't go. But if he gave me his blessing, it was almost as if Fate was forcing me to find my brother.

"Well, why didn't you say something earlier, boy?" George boomed. "I was worried about you, all alone in the world. It's always good to have relations, even if you don't get on with them. Because at the end of the day, you share a name; you share blood. It's good to know what they're up to."

"I suppose, sir," I said nervously. We were treading into dangerous territory. I'd never given him my real last name. Instead, he knew me as Stefan Pine. I'd chosen Pine not only because of its simplicity, but because I privately liked the idea of comparing myself to a pine tree: ever unchanging. It was a personal concession to my true nature. And so, I suppose, was Damon's personal choice of sobriquet.

"Take a week," George said.

"Thank you, but that won't be necessary on any count.

I'm only planning to call on my relatives for tea. And that's only if I can find them. But I do thank you," I said awkwardly.

"I'll tell you what," George said, leaning in toward me conspiratorially. "I'll bring you to my tailor, buy you some suits, and you can impress the hell out of your relatives."

"No, th—" I stopped myself. "Yes, I'd like that," I said firmly. After all, Damon was always so concerned with appearances that I wanted to beat him at his own game. I wanted him to see me as a man who'd made a proud life. Damon could lie and cheat his way into any social circle, but it took hard work to develop trust with humans, and I had done just that. Maybe I could even serve as a good example, a subtle reminder to Damon that he didn't have to live a life devoid of meaning.

"It's the least I can do, son," George said, before we lapsed again into silence. The only noise in our cabin was the rhythmic chugging of the train and the smacking of George's lips. I sighed. I felt suddenly constrained in our cabin, and wished I were in the barn on the edge of the Manor, alone with my thoughts.

"Quiet today, aren't you? You were last night, too," George said, breaking the silence. He wiped his mouth with a napkin and pulled the newspaper onto his lap.

"I suppose I am. I have a lot on my mind," I began. That might well have been the understatement of the year. This morning, all I'd been able to think about was Katherine. And now, the idea of Damon being so close was driving me to distraction.

George nodded, an understanding expression in his watery blue eyes.

"You don't need to tell me about it. I know all men have secrets, but please know that you have a friend in me," George said seriously. Although he knew only a skeleton of my history—that I'd left my father and America because I didn't want to marry the woman he'd chosen for me—something about his countenance made me want to open up to him a little bit more than I had.

"Of course, I'm not prying about your personal affairs," George said as he hastily rearranged the newspaper on his lap.

"No, you're not prying at all, sir. I thank you for your interest. The truth is, I have felt unsettled recently," I said finally, choosing my words carefully.

"Unsettled?" George asked in concern. "Is the job not to your liking? I know that it's a bit below your former station in America, but do know that I'm watching you, and I think that you really do have promise. Grow into yourself, get a few years under your belt, and I could see you going far. Perhaps you could even buy a piece of property yourself," George mused.

I shook my head quickly. "It's not the job," I said. "I'm

grateful for the opportunity, and am pleased to be on the farm. It's . . . I've been having nightmares about my past. I sometimes wonder . . . whether or not I can ever truly leave that part of my life behind. I sometimes think of my father's disappointment," I explained nervously. It was the most I'd ever opened up to any human except Callie. And yet I felt relieved saying the sentences, even though they didn't nearly explore the chasm-like depths of my problems.

"Growing pains." Mr. Abbott nodded sagely. "I remember having them, too, when my father was urging me to follow in his footsteps, eager to have someone carry on the name, his legacy. He was the one who told me that I'd marry Gertrude and that I'd run the farm. I did it, and I don't regret it. But what I do regret is that I never had a choice. Fact is, it's the life I would have chosen. But I think all men need to feel they're masters of their decisions." At this, Mr. Abbott smiled wistfully. "That's why I admire you, Stefan. Standing up for your principles and setting out on your own. This is a remarkable age. We're no longer a society based on who we are, but rather what we do. And everything I've seen you do has been exemplary," he said, taking a large bite of his scone, causing crumbs to scatter all over his shirt.

"Thank you," I said, feeling better than I had in a long time. Even if he didn't know everything about me, maybe there was truth in what George was saying—that what I chose to do was far more important than who I was or who I had been. As long as I continued to live like a productive member of society, then my Power would continue to ebb, until it was a nearly inaudible thrum in the background of my being. Meanwhile, I'd have so many other things to concern myself with: livestock, property, industry, money. A small smile played on my lips.

The train lurched forward, and tea splashed all over the front of George's jacket.

"Oh blast!" he murmured. "Would you mind holding this?" he asked, passing me his pages of the newspaper as he pulled his handkerchief out of his pocket to dab at the stain.

The bold font and exclamation points printed on the page immediately caught my eye.

Murder! screamed the headline. Underneath the text was a line drawing of a woman, her bodice ripped, blood seeping from her throat, her eyes half-open. Even though it was just a drawing, the image was gruesome. I leaned in for a closer look, as if compelled.

"Isn't that terrible?" George asked, his gaze falling on the paper. "Makes me glad to live far away from London."

I nodded, barely listening. I took the paper, the grimy newsprint smearing on my hands as I hastily scanned the article.

Woman of the night meets creature of dark-ness. The body of Mary Ann Nichols was found on the cobblestones of the Whitechapel area of London. Her throat was torn out and her innards removed. Could be connected to other deaths in the area. More details, from those who knew the victim. Page 23.

Not even caring about the curious way George was eyeing me, I turned to the page, the newspaper shaking in my hands. Yes, the murder was gruesome, but it was achingly familiar. I stared back at the line drawing on the front page of Mary Ann. Her blank face was tilted toward the sky, unimaginable horror evident in her unblinking eyes. That wasn't the work of a jilted lover or a desperate thief.

It was the work of a vampire.

Not only that, it was the work of a brutal, bloodthirsty vampire. In all my years, I hadn't seen or heard of any murder so gruesome—except for twenty years ago, when Lucius had massacred the Sutherland family. Damon had been there, too.

A shiver of fear ran up my spine. Wherever there were people, there were vampires. But most kept to themselves, and most, if they drank human blood, did so as quietly as possible: in shantytowns, from drunks on the street, simply compelling their friends and neighbors so they could regularly feed without anyone sensing a thing. But then, there were the Originals. Rumored to be descended directly from hell, the Originals had never had a soul, and thus had no memories of what it was like to live, to hope, to cry, to be human. What they did have was a relentless thirst for blood and a desire for destruction.

And if Klaus were here now . . . I shuddered to think of it, but just as quickly brushed the idea off. It was my overactive imagination at work. I was always assuming the worst, always assuming my secret was seconds away from being revealed. Always assuming I was doomed. No. More likely, this had been the work of a blood-drunk Damon who needed to be taught a lesson he should have learned a long time ago.

After all, Damon wasn't only bloodthirsty; he was fame hungry. He loved the society pages. Would it be that far of a leap for him to want to suddenly appear in the crime pages, too?

"Don't let that story scare you off from London," George said, laughing a bit too loudly. "This all took place in the slums. We won't be anywhere near there."

"It won't," I said firmly, my jaw set. I set the paper next to me. "In fact, I think I will take your offer and take the entire week off."

"As you wish," George said, leaning back into his chair, the murder story already off his mind. I glanced back down at the picture. The line illustration was gory and gruesome, the illustrator having clearly gone out of his way to vividly draw the innards falling out of the girl's body. Her face had been cut, too, but I kept glancing at her neck, wondering if two small, shodding nail–size holes were hidden underneath the gore.

The train whistled and I could see the vast expanse of London out the window. We were entering the city. I wanted the train to turn around and take me back to Abbott Manor. I wanted to run away, back to San Francisco or Australia, or somewhere where innocent people didn't get their throats ripped out by demons. Around us, porters bustled to get trunks and suitcases from the overhead bins. Across from me, George placed his hat on his head, glancing down to the paper.

"Can you imagine, that poor girl . . ." George trailed off.

The trouble was, I could imagine it all too well.

I could imagine Damon, flirting, allowing his hand to graze the woman's bodice. I pictured Damon, leaning in for a kiss as Mary Ann closed her eyes, ready for the brush of his lips. And then, I imagined the attack, a scream, her desperately clawing toward safety. And finally, I saw Damon, blood-drunk and sated, grinning in the moonlight.

"Stefan?"

"Yes?" I said gruffly, already on edge.

George eyed me curiously. The porter was holding open the door to our cabin.

"I'm ready," I said, steadying myself on the armrests as I stood up.

"You're shaking!" George said, laughing loudly. "But I promise you, London's in no way as frightening as the Ivinghoe woods. In fact, I wouldn't be surprised if you end up loving it. Bright lights, plenty of parties . . . why, if I were a younger man without responsibilities, I wouldn't be able to tear myself away from the place."

"Right," I said. His words had given me an idea. Until I'd found out who—or what—was loose in the city, London was where I was going to stay.

No matter what came, be it murderer, demon, or Damon, I was ready.

few hours later, my feet ached while my head kept spinning. My sense of duty kept me with George as we spent the morning shuttling between appointments and tailor fittings. I was now wearing linen pants and a white shirt from Savile Row, and had several more bags on my arms. Despite his generosity, I was desperate to escape George. All I could think about while trying on various clothes was the girl's blood-soaked, ripped bodice.

"Can I give you a lift to your relatives? You never did say where they lived," George said as he stepped off the street corner to nod his head at a passing carriage.

"No, that's quite all right," I said, cutting him off as the coach pulled up to the curb. The past few hours with George had been torturous, plagued with thoughts that would make his hair turn white and stand on end. I blamed Damon for poisoning what was supposed to have been nothing more than a day of pleasant diversions.

I glanced away so I wouldn't have to see George's bewildered expression. A few blocks away, I could just make out St. Paul's Cathedral. It was a structure I remembered sketching when I was a child and dreamt of being an architect. I'd always imagined it as being white and gleaming, but in reality it was constructed of a dingy gray limestone. The entire city felt dirty, a thin layer of grime coated my body, and the sun was covered by gray clouds.

Just then, the sky opened up and fat drops of rain landed on the pavement, as if reminding me this was my narrow chance to follow my instincts and flee from George.

"Sir?" the coach driver on the curb urged impatiently.

"I'll find my own way there," I said, sensing George's hesitation at leaving me. The coachman moved to escort George to the sleek black carriage.

"Enjoy yourself," George said, clambering up the steps of the coach. The coachman whipped his horse, and the carriage took off down the rain-soaked cobblestone streets.

I glanced around me. In the few minutes that George and I had been talking, the streets had become almost deserted. I shivered in my fine shirt. The weather perfectly matched my mood.

I raised my hand and hailed a coach of my own.

"Whitechapel," I said confidently, surprised as the words left my lips. I'd thought of going to the Journeyman to find Damon. And I would do that, eventually. But for now, I wanted to see for myself where the murder had taken place.

"Of course," the coachman said. And instantly, I was trotted into the maze of claustrophobic London streets.

After much back and forth with the coachman, he dropped me on the corner where the Tower Bridge was being constructed. Glancing around, I could see the Tower of London. It was smaller than I'd thought it would be, and the flags on its turrets didn't wave so much as droop in the constant trickle of rain. But I wasn't here to sightsee. I turned away from the river and onto Clothier Street, one of the many twisting, dirty, dank alleys that webbed through the city.

I quickly realized this part of town was vastly different than what I'd seen with George. Rotting vegetables cluttered the rain-slicked cobblestones. Thin, slanted buildings were shoddily thrown up almost on top of each other. The scent of iron was everywhere, although I couldn't tell whether the concentration of blood was from murder or simply from the mass of people forced to live in such close quarters. Pigeons hopped along the alleyways, but otherwise the area was deserted. I felt a shiver of fear creep up my spine as I hurried around the park and toward a tavern.

I walked inside and into nearly complete darkness. Only a few candles burned on the rickety tables. A small group of men were sitting along the bar. Meanwhile, several women were drinking in the corner. Their brightly colored dresses and festive hats were at odds with the gloomy surroundings, and gave them the look of caged birds at the zoo. No one seemed to be talking. I nervously adjusted the lapis lazuli ring on my finger, looking at the rainbow of refracted light the stone created on the gritty oak floor.

I sidled up to the bar and perched on one of the stools. The air was heavy and damp. I unbuttoned the top button of my shirt and loosened my tie to counter the stifling atmosphere. I wrinkled my nose in disgust. It wasn't the type of establishment I'd envision Damon frequenting.

"You one of them newspaper boys?"

I glanced up at the barkeep in front of me. One of his front teeth was gold, the other was missing, and his hair stuck out in wild gray tufts. I shook my head. *I just have a taste for blood.* The phrase popped into my mind. It was an off-color joke that Damon would have cracked. His favorite game was to almost give himself away, to see if anyone noticed. Of course they didn't. They were too busy being dazzled by Damon.

"Mate?" the barkeep asked curiously, plunking a filthy rag on the bar as he looked at me. "You one of them newspaper boys?" he repeated.

"No. And I think I might not be in the right place. Is the Journeyman nearby?" I asked, already knowing the answer.

"Ha! You 'avin' a laugh? The Journeyman is that right proper supper club. Only admits the toffs. Ain't our kind, and you won't get in neither, even with that fancy shirt. Only option is to drown your sorrows with some ale!" He laughed, displaying one of his gold molars in the back of his mouth.

"So the Journeyman club isn't close?" I asked.

"No, mate. Close to the Strand, near all them shows. Where the fancy folks go when they want to get wild. But they come here when they want to get wicked!" The barkeep laughed again as I glanced away, annoyed. I wasn't going to find Damon here. Unless . . .

"Beer, please. A dark ale," I said, suddenly inspired. Maybe I could get the barkeep to talk and find clues to who—or what—was responsible for Mary Ann's death. Because if it was Damon, either directly or indirectly, I'd finally teach him the lesson he should have learned long ago. I wouldn't kill him or stake him. But if it came down to it and I had him on the ground, at my mercy, would I hurt him?

Yes. I was immediately certain of my answer.

"What?" the barkeep asked, and I realized I'd spoken out loud.

"Just that I'd like that ale," I said, forcing a pleasant expression.

"All right, friend," the barkeep said amiably as he shuffled to one of the many taps that lined the back of the bar.

"Here you go." The barkeep pushed a glass of frothy brew toward me.

"Thank you," I said, tipping the glass toward me as though I were drinking. But I just barely let the liquid cross my lips. I needed to keep my wits.

"So you're not a newspaper boy, but you're not from around here, are you?" the bartender asked, leaning his elbows on the bar and gazing at me curiously with his bloodshot gray eyes.

Since I spoke to so few people, except for the Abbotts, I forgot that my Virginia accent instantaneously gave me away. "From America," I said briefly.

"And you came *here*? To Whitechapel?" the barkeep asked incredulously. "You know we have a murderer on the loose!"

"I think I read something about that in the paper," I said, trying to sound casual. "Who do they think it is?"

At this, the barkeep guffawed, slamming his beefy fist on the bar and almost causing my drink to tip over. "You hear that?" he called to the motley crew of men on the other side of the bar, who all seemed deep into their drinks. "He wants to know who the murderer is!"

At this, the other men laughed, too.

"I'm sorry?" I asked in confusion.

"I'm just having a laugh," the barkeep said jovially. "It's not some bloke who pinched a purse. This is an unholy killer. If any of us knew who it was, don't you think we'd go straight to Scotland Yard or the City of London police and let them know? It's bad for business! That monster has all our girls half-terrified!" He lowered his voice and glanced at the cluster of women in the corner. "And between you and me, I don't think any of us are safe. He's going for the girls now, but who's to say he won't go for us next? He takes his knife and like that, you're gone," he said, drawing his index finger across his throat for emphasis.

It doesn't have to be a knife, I wanted to say. I kept my gaze locked on the barkeep.

"But he doesn't start at the neck. Why, he cut that girl's innards right out. He likes to torture. He's looking for blood," he said.

At the mention of the word, my tongue automatically slicked over my teeth. They were still short and even. Human. "Do they have any leads? The murder sounds gruesome." I grimaced.

"Well . . ." The barkeep lowered his voice and raised his eyebrow at me. "First off, you promise you ain't from one of those papers? Not the *Guardian* or them other ones?"

I shook my head.

"Good. I'm Alfred, by the way," the barkeep said, reaching out his hand to me. I shook it, not offering my name in return. He continued, hardly noticing. "I know the life we live here doesn't seem prim and proper like what you might be used to across the ocean," he said, taking in my brand-new Savile Row outfit, which made me wildly overdressed for this establishment. "But we like our way of life. And our women," he added, waggling his salt-and-pepper eyebrows.

"The women . . ." I said. I remembered the article had said that the victim had been a woman of the night. Just the type of woman Damon had enjoyed at one point. I shivered in disgust.

"Yes, the women," Alfred said grimly. "Not the types of ladies you're going to meet at church, if you know what I mean."

"But the type of women you pray to meet in bed!" guffawed a ruddy-complexioned man two seats down, holding up his whiskey glass in a mock toast.

"None of that talk! We're a respectable establishment!" the barkeep said, a wicked spark in his eye. He turned his back to me and filled two glasses with several inches of amber liquid. He then turned and ceremoniously placed one in front of me.

"For you. Liquid courage. You need it around these parts, what with the murderer walking the streets," Alfred said, clinking his glass with mine. "Although my best advice is to stay here until sunrise. Maybe meet a nice lady. Better than meeting the Ripper."

"'The Ripper'?"

Alfred smiled. "That's what they're calling him. Because he doesn't just kill, he butchers. I'm telling you, stay here for your own protection."

"Thanks," I said uneasily. I wasn't sure if I wanted to stay. The smell of iron hadn't lessened in my time in the bar, and I was growing increasingly sure it was emanating from the walls and floor. The man in the corner kept staring at me, and I found myself staring back, trying to see any glimpse of fangs or blood-flecked chins. I could hear the women behind me whispering, and I wondered what they were discussing.

"Did Mary Ann . . . the most recent murder victim . . . did she ever drink here?" I asked hopefully. If I couldn't find Damon, then I'd just do the next best thing and find out all I could about Damon's victim.

"Rest in peace," the barkeep said reverentially. "She was a good girl. Came in from time to time, when she had enough pennies for gin. This ain't a charity, and the girls all knew they needed to pay the proper fee in order to spend time here. It was a system that worked out. The locals left the girls alone while they were out on the streets, unless they were striking a bargain. The girls respected the rules of the bar. And now, everything's fallen apart. If I ever find the bloke who did it, I'll rip his throat out," Alfred said savagely, pounding his fist against the table.

"But did she leave with anyone, or was there ever a man you saw her with?" I pressed.

"I saw her with a lot of men over the years. But none that stood out. Most of 'em were the blokes who worked down by the docks. Rough types, but none that would do that. Those blokes aren't looking for any trouble, just a good pint and a good girl. Besides, she left by herself that night. Sometimes, when there's too many girls here, they go out to the streets. Less competition," he explained, noticing my confused expression. "But before she left, she'd had a good night here. She had some gin, a few laughs. Was wearing a new hat she was so proud of. Felt like it drew the men over to her. The good kind, too, not the ones who only pretend to have money. I wish she'd stayed, God bless her," Alfred said, raising his eyes piously to the ceiling.

"And her body . . ." I asked.

"Well, now, the body was found in Dutfield Park. It's where the ladies sometimes go when they can't afford a room. I don't say nothin', whatever goes on outside the premises ain't my business. But that's where he got her and slit her throat."

I nodded, my mind racing back to one of the many over-grown squares of grass that dotted the area. The weeds, garbage, and peeling paint of the iron fences surrounding the parks all made the area seem more dismal than simple city squares.

"And if you *are* one of them newspaper boys, then I didn't say nothing. What's your name anyway, boy?" Alfred asked.

"Stefan," I said, taking a huge swig of whiskey. It did nothing to calm the dread in my stomach. A soulless killer was loose, and he would stop at nothing.

"Well, Stefan, welcome to Whitechapel," he said, raising his second glass. "And remember, better whiskey down your throat than the murderer on it."

I smiled tightly as I held up a glass to my new friend.

"Here, here!" one of the drunk men at the other end of the bar said. I smiled at him, fervently hoping that too many whiskeys drunk at the pub wouldn't lead them all to their doom.

The devil you know is better than the devil you don't. The phrase floated into my mind. It was one that Lexi would often invoke, and it was one I'd only found to be more and more true as time passed. Because as horrid and soulless as the crime was, if Damon had done it, at least I wouldn't have any other vampires to worry about. But the longer I stayed at the bar, the more another thought tugged at my brain: What if it wasn't Damon, but another vampire?

Down at the other end of the bar, Alfred had drifted

into conversation with a few of the other customers. Rain pelted against the windows, and I was reminded of the fox den at the far side of the Abbotts' farm. Entire families of beasts huddled there, waiting for the moment when they thought it was safe to head into the forest. The unlucky ones would be hit by a hunter's bullet.

I glanced around again. A woman in a lilac dress allowed her hand to slide down a man's shoulder. The real question was, who were the foxes and who were the hunters? All I could hope was that I was a hunter.

4

The longer I spent at the pub, the more crowded it became—but there was no sign of Damon. I told myself I was staying to try to find more clues. But the truth was, I didn't know what I could do. Stand outside the supper club? Plod up and down the streets of London until I happened to run into Damon? Sit in Dutfield Park myself until another attack happened? The last was the one idea I kept toying with. But it was ludicrous. For one, why would the murderer strike twice at the same place? For another, what would I do if I saw the murder? Scream? Call the police? Find a stake and hope for the best? None of the options seemed ideal. And if the murderer *wasn't* Damon . . . well, then I could be dealing with a fiend from hell. I was strong, but not that strong. I needed a plan.

I watched as customers poured in. Each seemed seedier than the last, but all were reassuringly human. Some men, the ones with cracked nails and dirty shirts, had obviously just gotten off their construction jobs, while others, reeking of cologne and furtively glancing at the women at the corner tables, were clearly there to consort with ladies of the night. And indeed, I couldn't help but notice each time a garishly garbed woman stepped into the tavern, the crowd surveyed her as if they were gamblers at the racetrack sizing up the horses.

These women stood in stark contrast to the serving girl who seemed in charge of the entire room. She couldn't have been older than sixteen or seventeen, and skinny as a jaybird, but every time I saw her, her arms were laden with plates and pint glasses. At one point, I watched her hurry toward the kitchen, but before she got there, she paused to clear the plates from a nearby table. All that remained on one plate were a few scraps of meat, some potatoes, and a half-eaten roll. She stared hard at the plate, before cautiously grabbing the meat and slipping it into her pocket. Then, she crammed the roll into her mouth, her cheeks puffing like a chipmunk's, before scurrying back to the kitchen.

I closed my eyes. I'd long ago given up praying, and I didn't think any sort of God would want to hear my requests, but I did wish that no matter what happened, that this helpless seventeen-year-old would stay far, far away from Dutfield Park. Or, for that matter, any blood-thirsty vampire.

"Lookin' for a good time, love?" A woman with blond curled hair and crooked teeth perched on the wooden seat opposite me. Her white bosom was overflowing from her bodice.

"No. Sorry," I said roughly, waving my hand away. A memory from New Orleans flooded back to me. It had been in my first few weeks as a vampire, when I'd been bloodthirsty and bullheaded, and had dragged Damon to a house of ill repute. There, I'd feasted on a young girl, sure that no one would notice or care that she'd disappeared. I couldn't even remember her name now, and I wondered if I'd ever even bothered to learn it in the first place. It was details like those that would cause me to sink into the depths of misery, and here, in this dank tavern, I couldn't escape these split-second flashbacks. All of them were reminders that no matter what I did, and no matter who I helped, I'd never do enough good deeds to wash away all the blood I was responsible for—and would be for eternity—off my hands. All I could do was try. And I would do anything to ensure that these women would not die at the hands of a demon.

I glanced back down at the paper, now creased and smudged from my hands. I could almost recite every word of the article, and none of it seemed to make sense. Why had the killer just left her like that? It was almost as if he'd wanted her to be found. But if the killer had wanted *her* to be found, he had to be very, very careful to cover his own tracks.

"What would you like to eat, love?" a lilting voice asked. I looked up to see the skinny, wide-eyed serving girl. She was wearing a tattered and stained rose-colored dress that was covered by a filthy white apron. She had wide blue eyes and long auburn hair that hung in a single braid down her back. A smattering of freckles dusted her angular face, and her skin was as smooth and pale as ivory. She kept nervously biting her lips, a habit that reminded me a bit of Rosalyn, my fiancée back in Virginia. But even Rosalyn's extreme caution hadn't prevented her from getting killed by a vampire. My heart went out to this girl.

"Whatever you recommend," I said, putting down the paper. "Please," I added. My stomach was growling, but what I most wanted wasn't on any menu.

"Well, a lot of people have ordered the fish . . ." she said, trailing off. Even from where I was sitting, I could hear her heart beating, as fast and lightly as a swallow's.

"That sounds fine," I said. I tried not to think of the dwindling coins in my pocket.

"Yes, sir," the girl said, turning quickly on her heel.

"Wait!" I called.

"Yes?" she asked, concern in her eyes. She looked so much like Oliver when he was worried that Mrs. Duckworth would scold him. There was something about the deliberate way she spoke, her ultra-cautious movements, and those wide, seeking eyes that made me feel she'd seen or heard something in connection to the murder. It was more than just an air of teenage self-consciousness.

She seemed haunted.

"Yes?" she asked again, her eyes furrowing. "You don't have to order the fish if you don't like. We also have steak-and-kidney pie . . ."

"No, fish is fine," I said. "But may I ask you a question?"

She glanced at the bar. Once she saw Alfred was deep in conversation with a patron, she tiptoed a few steps closer.

"Sure."

"Do you know Count DeSangue?" I asked steadily.

"Count DeSangue?" she repeated. "We don't get counts here, no."

"Oh," I said, disappointed. Of course they didn't. She kept glancing between me and Alfred.

"Did you know . . . the girl who was murdered?" I asked. I felt like I was at a church social in Mystic Falls, wondering which cousin of Clementine's knew which cousin of Amelia's.

"Mary Ann? No." The girl set her mouth in a tight line and took a step away from me. "I'm not like that."

"Violet?" Alfred called from the bar.

"Yes, sir!" Violet squeaked. "He don't have to eat my head off," she murmured under her breath. She pulled a pad of paper from her pocket and hastily scribbled on it, as if she were taking down an order. Then, she put the paper on the table and hurried away.

> *Are you the police? My sister is gone. Cora*
> *Burns. Please help. I think she may have been*
> *killed.*

I shuddered as I read the words.

Moments later, the girl reemerged from the kitchen, a steaming plate in her hand.

"Here's your food, sir," she said, curtseying as she placed the plate on the table. A grayish slab of fish was covered in heavy gelatinous cream.

"I'm not the police," I said, staring into her eyes.

"Oh. Well, I thought you might have been. You were just asking so many questions, you see," the girl said, color appearing high on her cheekbones. "I'm sorry, I shouldn't have troubled you." She took a few suspicious steps away from me, and I realized she probably thought I was just like the other louts who frequented the bar, who only offered initial kindness and interest in order to have their way with her later.

"Wait!" I said. "I might be able to help you. But can we talk?"

"I don't know," she said. Her eyes darted nervously around the tavern.

"Have a seat," I said.

Nervously, she perched on the stool. I nudged the plate over toward her. "Would you like it?" I asked, locking eyes with her. I could hear her heart beating faster against her rib cage. She must have been starving. "Here," I added encouragingly, pushing the plate closer to her.

"I don't need charity," she said insistently, a hint of pride in her voice. Still, I noticed her eyes continue to dart from my dinner to me.

"Please take it. You look hungry, and I'd like you to have it."

She eyed the plate suspiciously. "Why?"

"Because I'm not hungry anymore. And it sounds like you're having a hard day," I said gently. "My name's Stefan. And you are . . . ?"

"V-V-Violet," she said finally. She picked up a fork and took one bite, then another, of the fish. Catching me staring, she picked up a napkin and shyly dabbed her mouth. "You're a good man, Stefan."

"I try to be." I shrugged as I gave her a small smile. She was quieter than Callie had been, but had far more spunk than Rosalyn did. I'd inwardly cheered when she told Alfred off under her breath. She had pluck, and I just knew *that*, more than anything else, would save her. "So about Cora—"

"Shhh!" Violet interrupted me.

I turned over my shoulder and saw Alfred storm out from around the bar toward our table. Before I could react, he'd grabbed Violet's long hair and yanked it, causing her to yelp.

"What are you doing, girl?" he growled, his face showing none of the earlier jocularity he'd had behind the bar. "Begging for food like a mongrel?"

"No, sir, let her go. I invited her to dine with me!" I said, quickly standing up. I clenched my hands into fists and stared into Alfred's beady eyes.

"She's not good enough to dine with my customers. Out on the street is where you belong," Alfred yelled, his voice rising as he ignored my protests. "You're worse than them ladies over there," he said, jutting his chin at the trio of women who still seemed to be surveying the crowd. "At least they've got something to offer," he said, his face turning red.

"Please, sir!" Violet said, her entire frame shaking. Alfred loosened his grip on her hair, but his mouth was still set in a firm line. "I'll do anything. Please don't take away my job."

"What job? Your sister doesn't come in, so she sends

you. You're too small to lift anything and not pretty enough to keep the customers coming back. So I give you one task. Take the orders and bring them to the cook. And you can't even do that!" Alfred boomed.

"Please!" I interjected desperately, placing a hand on his arm. I'd only meant for the gesture to stop him from grabbing Violet again, but in the moment, I'd forgotten my strength. His arm flew back, propelling him away from Violet.

I watched as he staggered backward into the table. The plate of fish landed upside down on the floor with a clatter. Violet looked terrified and I realized that the normal din had quieted to a churchlike hush. All eyes were on us.

Alfred scowled at me, rubbing his arm, as if debating whether or not to start a fight. "Well," he said, clearing his throat.

"I apologize, but she wasn't doing anything wrong. I asked her to join me. I offered her my meal," I said in a smooth, low voice. I was furious, but I needed to control my temper. "Do you understand me?" I asked.

"Yes," Alfred said, jerking his gaze away. He turned toward Violet.

"That true, girl?" he asked roughly.

"Yes," Violet said in a small voice. "And I said no, but you say the customer is always right, and I thought that you'd want me to do what he said, so . . ."

Alfred raised his hand to cut her off and turned toward me. "Now I don't know what you were trying to do, but Violet is not on offer," Alfred said stiffly, still rubbing his arm. "If you wish to meet a lady, there are ones I'd be delighted to introduce to you. I know you're not from around here, but this is my bar and my rules. Are we agreed? Now you," he said, turning to Violet. "Out!" He pointed toward the door.

"Love, I can keep you warm tonight, if you know what I mean!" one of the bar patrons yelled as he reached to pinch her rear end. Another man followed suit, pawing at her. But she stared straight ahead, even as tears fell down her cheeks, and walked toward the front door.

"It's for the best," Alfred said roughly, crossing his beefy arms over his chest as the door closed with a thud. "You don't run this bar. I do. And she was bothering you."

"She *wasn't* bothering me!" I said, angrily throwing a few shillings on the table before stepping menacingly toward him. A flicker of fear registered in Alfred's face. I considered taking my frustrations out on him, but it was no use. Violet was gone. And every second she was outside meant she was in danger.

I stormed out of the bar without a second glance and walked into darkness. Only a few stars peeked through the tattered gray blanket of the London evening. I pulled out my pocket watch, a gift from Winfield Sutherland back in New York. After all those years, it still worked. It was nearly midnight. The witching hour.

A sliver of a moon hung high in the sky, and a layer of fog, so thick I could feel dewy condensation on my skin, swirled around the dilapidated buildings surrounding me. I cocked my head like a hunting dog. I could hear laughter emanating from the tavern, but no matter how hard I tried, I couldn't hear the *ba-da-bump*, *ba-da-bump* gallop of Violet's heartbeat.

I'd lost her.

I glanced around, trying to get my bearings. Even though the tavern had been bustling, the rest of the area seemed desolate. It reminded me a bit of some of the towns I'd seen when I'd taken a train from New Orleans to New York City—places so decimated by the war that no one was left.

I walked through the maze of streets, unsure of where I was going. I wanted to find Violet. I had some money from my wages, and I was sure I could settle the price of a rooming house for her. But how could I find her in an unfamiliar city with streets and alleys that seemed to number in the millions? It was impossible.

After a few moments, I came to a park. Or rather, I came to a patch of greenery that at one point might have been a park. Now, the grass was yellowed, the trees were sickly, paint was peeling from the wrought-iron benches, and none of the gas lamps were lit. I shivered. If this was Dutfield Park, then it was the ideal place for a murder.

I tilted my head. I could hear heartbeats—of rabbits, and squirrels, and even a fox—but then I heard it: *ba-da-bump, ba-da-bump.*

"Violet!" I called, my voice cracking. I easily jumped over the peeling fence and ran toward the woods in the center of the park. "Violet!" I called again, the *ba-da-bump* getting closer.

And then, a shriek pierced the air, followed by deafening silence.

"Violet!" I yelled, my fangs bulging. I pelted through the trees as if my feet were running on air, not gravel, expecting to see Damon feasting on Violet's neck. Damon, turning toward me with blood dripping down his chin. Damon arching his eyebrow and greeting me with the one word that made my brain almost explode with anger . . .

"Help!" a girl's voice screamed.

"Violet!" I called, tearing through the trees, in one direction, then another, listening wildly for the *ba-da-bump, ba-da-bump* of her heart. And then I saw her, standing shakily near a dark streetlight. Her face was as white as her apron, but she was alive. There was no blood.

"Violet?" I asked, slowing down to a walk. My feet crunched against the dry underbrush. The path in the woods had obviously, in happier times, been designed for a

Sunday afternoon stroll. A small brick building, most likely a groundskeeper's cottage, long since abandoned, stood at the crest of a gentle hill. Violet was staring at it, her mouth formed into an *O* of horror.

I followed her gaze, the sliver of the moon providing just enough light that I could see red letters written on the side of the building, each oxidized character standing out against the muted brick as if it were illuminated from behind by candlelight:

SALVATORE—I SHALL HAVE MY REVENGE

I glanced at the words, feeling as though the wind had been knocked out of me. This was a challenge, as real as if I'd been dealt a blow by an unseen hand. Someone was after us. And that someone wasn't Damon. Worse still, what if *Damon* was the one in trouble? I wouldn't put it past my brother to find himself at the center of a deadly vampire disagreement. After all, that's what had happened in New York.

I blinked. I'd only seen a gruesome message like that once in my infinite lifetime—at the Sutherlands' in New York, when Lucius, Klaus's minion, was fulfilling the Original's desire for vengeance against me and my brother. Twenty years ago, we'd just narrowly escaped him. Could he be back for more?

If Klaus had returned, I owed it to my brother to warn him. Suddenly everything—my terrifying dreams, my unsettled feelings—made sense. Damon was in trouble. And like it or not, I'd heard the message and come running. No matter what, my connection to the murder was no longer just a hunch—I was a part of this now. There was no going back.

"Help! Anyone!" Violet shrieked. She was starting to panic, her eyes wide.

I ran toward her and clapped my hand over her mouth to keep her from crying out again. I may have been hunting Damon, but now I was being hunted. Together, we were just two foxes, desperately darting through the city, unsure whether the hunter in charge of our fates was in front of us or behind us or lying in wait, ready to strike when we least expected it.

In that moment, staring at the bloody message, time stood still. Or rather, time flew backward, back twenty years and across the ocean, until I was in the formal drawing room of the Sutherlands' Central Park mansion, surrounded by carnage, gazing at a similarly garish, violent message.

Damon had been by my side back then, and it was at that moment I realized that the two of us were truly just babes in the woods, boys masquerading as monsters. When we saw the message written in the Sutherlands' blood, we'd finally grasped that evil beyond our imaginations existed.

And it had only gotten worse. When Lucius, the minion of Klaus, had found and captured Damon

*and me, he'd entombed us in a mausoleum as if
we were buried alive, heedless of our cries. Klaus
and his ilk were Originals, creatures straight from
hell who didn't even have the smallest memory of
human kindness, and, as such, there was no end
to their evil. And now one of them was after me.*

*But for a moment, I felt something else inside
me. It was a flickering sensation, so subtle and
foreign I barely noticed it. Until I realized what it
was. It was hope.*

*This time, I wasn't unprepared. I was older,
wiser, stronger. I could stop them.*

I would make sure of that.

"Violet!" I said sharply, my hand still firm against her
mouth. She stared at me with wild, unseeing eyes.

"I'm Stefan. From the bar. You can trust me. You *have*
to trust me," I said urgently. The edge of the park was only
a hundred yards away. It would only take a few seconds
to get out using vampire speed. I felt unsafe here. I didn't
feel much safer in London's claustrophobic streets, but at
least there, with pedestrians nearby, the killer would be
less likely to strike. "We need to leave."

She took a deep breath, but continued to struggle
against my grip. "Violet, listen to me," I said, summon-
ing my Power. I heard a snap of a twig in the forest and I

jumped. We had no time. Klaus could be anywhere. "Violet, trust me. You will be quiet, and you will listen to me. Is that understood?"

I felt my thoughts reach her mind, and I sensed the moment when her brain seemed to yield. I nodded to try to speed the process.

Then I saw a flicker in her eyes. I wasn't sure if my compulsion had worked or if it was exhaustion, but I had to believe it. I took my hand off her mouth and she blinked dazedly at me.

"You'll be safe with me. We have to leave the park. I'll carry you," I explained as I picked Violet up and draped her over my shoulders. I sped out of the woods and darted into the streets. Faster and faster, I ran on the uneven cobblestones, always following the Thames River, its glassy surface reflecting the moon and the stars. I ran through alleys and back streets until we reached a part of the city with plenty of gas lamps and pedestrians. Even at this late hour, they were walking the streets as though it were broad daylight. I allowed myself to stop, ducking under an awning. Despite the heat that still clung to the late-summer night, the women had furs draped over their bare shoulders while the men were wearing top hats and three-piece suits. Dozens of marquees lit up either side of every street.

I allowed Violet to slip off my shoulders and the two

of us stood, facing each other, as throngs of pedestrians passed on either side of us.

Immediately, Violet began to panic again, and I could tell she wanted to scream, with only my compulsion holding her back.

"Shhh!" I tried to calm her. "Shhh!" I said again, rubbing her shoulders. A few passersby turned to stare.

"Listen to me," I whispered, hoping that she'd take a hint from my lowered voice. "You're safe. I'm your friend."

She continued to sniffle. Her eyes were red-rimmed, and her hair was tangled in thick vines around her freckled face. "You're safe," I said, not breaking eye contact. She nodded slowly.

"You have to trust me. Can you do that, Violet? Remember, I'm a good man. You said so yourself." I fished in my pocket and pulled out a white handkerchief, just purchased from the tailor. It seemed like a lifetime ago.

I handed it to her and Violet whimpered noisily. The few passersby who'd stopped to watch us on the street continued walking, obviously satisfied that nothing untoward was happening between us.

I let go of her, not wanting to compel her for a second longer than necessary. She seemed so innocent that I felt guilty for doing it, even though I knew it was for her own good.

"St-St-Stefan . . ." she said, gasping for breath. "The

blood . . . and the words . . . was it the murderer?" Her voice broke into another wail. She was bordering on hysteria again.

"Shhh," I said, trying to make my voice sound like the soothing whoosh of waves I'd heard on the boat to Britain. "Shhh," I repeated.

Violet sucked in her breath. "What if he has my sister? She's been missing since yesterday, and I haven't heard from her. And I thought . . ."

"He doesn't," I said firmly, wishing I knew that were true.

"I can't go back to the tavern," Violet said in a small voice.

"There's no need," I said, gently holding her wrist and pulling her toward the side of the street. In the dim light of a gas lamp she looked pale and drawn, and I felt a surge of sympathy toward her. Right now, I was all she had. "We'll find you a place to sleep," I decided, turning my mind back to the matters at hand.

"But I've got no money," she said worriedly, her hands searching the pockets of her pinafore.

"Don't worry. You're with me," I said, glancing around at the lights that cut through the fog, searching for a hotel or tavern where we could take our bearings. A sign down the street caught my eye: CUMBERLAND HOTEL.

"Let's go there," I suggested as I led Violet across the

street. Together, we marched up the red carpet–covered marble steps and through the gilt-gold doors, held open by a butler in a three-piece suit. With Lexi, I'd spent some time at some of the finest hotels in America, but I quickly realized that this establishment was on an entirely different level. Fresh-cut flowers were placed in large crystal bowls on every polished, gleaming surface, and the chandeliers were heavy gold. The man behind the desk glanced suspiciously at Violet and me.

"May I help you, sir?" he asked, his voice barely containing his disgust at her disheveled appearance. Out of the corner of my eye, I saw a woman in a silver chiffon gown with a train glide up the stairs, followed by two servants. At the corner bar, two men in tuxedos were draining crystal tumblers of whiskey. I felt my shoulders relax. For now, we were safe.

"Sir?" the man behind the desk prompted.

"Yes." I cleared my throat. I needed to pull myself together to successfully compel him. It was one thing to compel someone who was half-starved and hysterical, and entirely another to compel a man in charge of his wits.

"Yes, you may help me," I said, confidently stepping up to the marble-topped counter while a terrified Violet trailed behind me. The lighting in the old-fashioned lobby was dim, with dozens of candelabra giving the room in an orange glow that cast large, hulking shadows on the walls.

Every time one of the shadows moved, I glanced over my shoulder.

"What may I do for you?" the man behind the desk prompted pointedly.

I squared my shoulders and looked into his beady, gray eyes. I concentrated on the pupils, allowing my gaze to center in until the blackness was all I could see. "We need a room."

"I'm sorry. We don't have any rooms available for tonight," the man said.

"I know it's short notice, but there must be a room reserved for when royalty come to visit. My wife and I need that room," I said.

"But Stefan!" Violet squeaked behind me. Without breaking eye contact, I gently placed my foot on top of hers in warning. I'd learned the trick of asking for a room reserved for VIP guests from Lexi. It always worked.

"The *best* room," I added for emphasis.

"The best room," he said slowly, shuffling some papers. "Of course. The Queen Victoria Suite. She's stayed there, you know," he said.

"Good. Well then I imagine we shall love it just as much as she did," I said, affecting a bit of a British accent.

"I do hope so, Mr. . . . um . . ."

"Pine," I said, using the first name that popped into my head. *Hurry up*, I thought under my breath. I knew I was quickly losing Power. After all, it had been almost a day since I'd eaten properly. "I shall need the room for at least a week," I added, hoping that I'd be far away before the week was out.

The man behind the desk nodded, and I smiled. I could still compel. I still had my Power. And I had twenty years of wisdom under my belt. I hadn't been ready to fight Klaus back then, but now it would be different.

"The porter shall show you your room," the man said. "And do you and your wife have any bags?"

I shook my head. Instantaneously, a tall, morose-looking butler walked around the desk and held out his arm to Violet.

"And sir?" I said, lowering my voice so no one, not even Violet, would hear. "Just put it on my account."

"Of course, sir," the desk clerk said, sliding a heavy iron key across the counter. "Enjoy your stay."

I smiled tersely and followed the porter and Violet up the sweeping staircase, winding past floors until we stopped in front of a white door. It was the only door on the entire level.

"Allow me," the porter said, taking the key from my hand and putting it in the lock. He grandly swung the door open, then, placing a silver candleholder on a cherry-wood desk, quickly set to work lighting the various lamps in the room.

"Oh!" Violet trembled, clapping her hands to her mouth.

"Thank you." I nodded to the porter, pulling a shilling from my threadbare pocket. He took it in his palm and eyed me curiously. I hadn't compelled him, and I knew the fact we were practically wearing rags, and were without luggage, piqued his curiosity.

The door creaked shut and I locked it behind him.

"Stefan?" Violet asked tentatively, staring around the room in wonder. She walked in a circle, touching the heavy velvet curtains, the oak desk, and the floral-papered walls, as if scarcely believing any of it was real.

"We're okay now. It's late, we should both get some rest," I said, gesturing toward the enormous bed in the center of the main room. "I'll just be in the next room. We can talk in the morning."

"Goodnight, Stefan. And thank you." She gave me a small, tired smile and stepped toward the bed. I closed the door with a click and settled onto a couch in the adjacent room, which was set up like a sitting room. And sit I did. My mind reeled, and I couldn't even begin to pick apart the questions I needed to focus on. What was I going to do with Violet? What could I do about Klaus? Or Lucius? Part of me simply wanted to pick up and head back to Ivinghoe, where the only thing I had to concern myself with was a cow that had kicked over the pasture fence. But another part of me knew I was bound to London. I was a part of this now. Until I solved the mystery of the murder, more people would get killed.

Terrifying thoughts kept turning in my head as night turned into day. Below me, the well-lit streets looked orderly and tidy: modern civilization at its finest. Even the rain-slicked surface looked somehow stately. But I knew it was all an illusion. Vampires struck anywhere, and just because this one had chosen the bad part of town didn't mean he wouldn't come here next.

Finally, the sun rose, burning off some of the thick clouds. The door creaked open, providing a much-needed interruption from my endlessly cycling thoughts.

"Hello?" I called hesitantly. I still felt on edge, and any noise caused a tingling in my gums, a subtle reminder that I was ready to fight at any moment.

"Stefan?" Violet said shyly, stepping into the room. Her red hair was pulled up in a bun on top of her head and her pinafore looked brighter than it had last night, making me guess she'd rinsed it in the opulent washroom. Her eyes were sparkling and her hair, I realized now in the light, was flecked with gold.

"Violet," I said, rising unsteadily to my feet. I ignored the hunger pangs in my stomach.

"Did you sleep?" Violet asked, settling onto the couch

and pulling her legs underneath her. I crossed the room and perched on the wooden desk chair opposite her.

I shook my head. "I had a lot on my mind," I said, clenching and unclenching my jaw. Every part of my body ached, although whether it was from the terror of last night or from our flight through London, I couldn't tell.

"I did, too," Violet confessed, sighing sadly as she cradled her head in her hands. "My sister . . . I'm so worried about her," she said finally.

"What happened to her?" I asked. Just hours ago, I was hoping Damon wasn't responsible for these deaths and disappearances. Now, I was hoping against hope he was. Damon had been known to compel women for his own amusement. If he'd done it to Cora, well, that would mean she was still alive. But if Klaus or Lucius had found her . . . I shivered.

"That's the very thing. I just don't know. She went to work at the Ten Bells two nights ago, and then she didn't come home. Then the murder happened . . . and everyone said . . ." Violet's lips twisted into a grimace, but she forged ahead. "They said that maybe she didn't come home because she went home with someone else. That she went home with a man, like some of the girls at the tavern do," Violet said, a crimson flush crossing her face. "But Cora isn't like that. And I'm not like that. I tried telling Alfred and an

officer who came in that Cora wouldn't have just gone off
with someone, that she was missing. But they didn't do anything," she said sadly, knitting her fingers together as she
stared at the ground.

"Why not?" I asked. I felt angry that no one was taking
Violet's concerns seriously. After all, she was just an innocent young girl, worried about her sister.

Violet shook her head. "The police said they can't do
anything until they find a body. They said she's a grown
woman and she can go where she pleases. I'm just so worried." Violet sighed.

"But if Cora were killed . . ." I began, trying to reassure
her with the conclusion I'd come to last night, "surely her
body would have been found."

"Don't *say* that!" Violet said sharply. "I'm sorry," she
added instantly. "I just hate hearing it. But yes, you're right.
If she was killed, they would have found . . . something,"
she said, shuddering. I nodded, silently agreeing. "But I
haven't heard anything. No one has. And that's just the
thing. She wouldn't have left without telling me. It isn't
like her."

"People change," I said helplessly, unsure what I could
say to try to comfort Violet.

"But Cora is my *sister*," Violet insisted. "We came over
here together six months ago. We'd never leave each other.
We're all we have in the world. We're blood."

"Where did you come from?" I asked, trying not to cringe at the word *blood*.

"Ireland," Violet said with a faraway gaze in her eyes. "Just a tiny town near Donegal. All it has is a church and a pub, and we both knew we couldn't stay there. Our parents did, too. Our father used everything he had to send us both here. Thought we'd marry, start families, never have to worry about going hungry . . ." Violet laughed a short, harsh bark that was so at odds with her sweet and innocent personality that I flinched. Despite her youthful appearance, she'd obviously led a rough life.

"And life didn't work out as planned," I said slowly. I could relate all too well.

Violet nodded, her expression bereft. "We thought we'd become actresses or singers. Well, I did. Cora did it more for a laugh. But I thought I'd get a part in the chorus of a show," she said thoughtfully. "And we tried, but we just got laughed out of the auditions. Then we thought that we could become shop girls. But as soon as anyone saw our clothes and heard our accents, they turned us away. We just kept walking and walking around the city, talking to anyone with an Irish accent. We finally met a girl, Mary Francis, who was cousins with a boy from our town. She worked at the tavern and told us she'd put a word in with Alfred. So we went, and Alfred liked Cora right away. But he said I looked too young. So I was put to work in the back as a scullery maid."

I must have grimaced, because a shadow of a smile crossed Violet's face.

"I felt worse for Cora. She used to have to flirt with Alfred. I know that's why he gave me a job, and why he let us rent a room. We'd get into bed at the end of a long night and tell each other stories about our day. She always said that working in the tavern could maybe be helpful for me one day. It's all studying characters and seeing how they interact. She thought if we made enough money, we could try again to be actresses. She never gave up."

"Did you?" I asked gently.

"Well, at a certain point, you realize dreams are just that—dreams. I think sometimes that I should just accept it. Do you know this is the closest I've gotten to the theater since I've been here?" she asked, gazing out the window at the marquees nearby. "And Cora . . ." She shook her head. "Where is she?" she cried, burying her face in her tiny hands. "Things are so desperate that I can't even begin to think about them. I just keep hoping Cora found a better life. Not in heaven. I mean, here. A better life here. And maybe she didn't tell me because she didn't want me to be hurt or jealous? It's the only thing I can think of," Violet said, still hiding her face with her hands.

"I know Cora's safe." Of course I didn't know that at all, but as soon as I said it, I saw Violet's shoulders relax. I felt sad for this girl, who truly didn't have a friend in the world.

I wished that I could help her. Suddenly, I had an idea.

"Here's what I can do," I said. "I can get you the job back, and I can also guarantee Alfred won't bother you. I can't promise the job will be ideal, but I can promise that it will be better than it was before," I said, knowing I'd have to find somewhere to feed before I would be able to effectively compel Alfred.

"Thank you," Violet said. A slight smile played on her lips. "In my country, on Saint Stephen's Day we honor the saint who protects the poor," she said. "And I think it's come early for me this year. Thank you, Saint Stefan."

I looked away, uncomfortable with her adoration. If she only knew my true nature, she'd be praying to her saint for protection from me. "Don't thank me. Just stay here and rest up. I'll go and speak with Alfred and find out what I can about Cora," I said.

"I should come," Violet said definitively, rising to her feet.

I shook my head. "It won't be safe."

"But if it's not safe, then what about you?" Violet asked in a small voice. "I shan't forgive myself if anything happened to you while you were out on account of me."

"Nothing will happen to me," I said, wishing that were true. "I'm not afraid to fight. But I won't have to. Everything will be fine."

"It's funny, but I believe everything you say," Violet

said dreamily. "But I don't even know you. Who *are* you?"

"I'm Stefan Sa—I'm Stefan," I said. I refrained from saying my last name, worried it might scare her because of last night's message. "I'm from America. And I know what it's like to be alone. I left my family. It's hard."

Violet nodded. "Do you miss them?"

"Sometimes. I worry about them," I said. That was true.

"Well, then I suppose we're kindred spirits," Violet said. "You truly saved me. I don't know what I would have done in the park, there, by myself."

"Did you . . . see anyone?" I asked. It was the question I hadn't asked her last night. But now, in the light of day, I needed to know.

She shook her head. "I don't think so. It was so dark, and I could barely see in front of me. But I felt the wind pick up, and then I saw the trees moving. When I glanced over, I saw that awful message. And I knew it was written in blood. I felt something. I felt . . ." She shuddered.

"What did you feel?" I asked gently.

Violet sighed, distress obvious on her face. "I felt like I was surrounded by evil. Something was there. I thought I was going to be attacked, and then you came and—"

"I brought you here," I said quickly. I knew exactly how she felt. It was a feeling I suffered from back in New York, when I was sure Klaus was near. I fumbled in my pocket. "And now, your Saint Stefan has one more thing for you. Take this," I said, pressing a pendant into her hand. It was a vial of vervain on a gold chain.

"What is it?" she asked, swinging the pendant back and forth. It caught the flickering light of the candle on the table.

"A good luck charm," I said. Vervain was poisonous to me, and I could still feel its effects through the glass barrier of the vial. But I carried it everywhere. So far, I'd never had to use it. And I only hoped that Violet wouldn't have to, either.

"I need luck," Violet said, clasping the pendant around her neck. As long as she had that, she couldn't be compelled, not even by me. We now were fully bound to each other by trust alone.

"So do I," I said.

And then, she stood up on her tiptoes and allowed her lips to graze my cheek. "To luck," she whispered in my ear.

I grinned at her. Hell itself may have been hunting these streets, but at least I had a friend. And as I'd learned in my long life, that was no small thing.

6

In the light of day, the winding London streets didn't seem nearly as intimidating as they had during my wild run the night before. Carriages filled the roads, peddlers on the corners hawked everything from flowers to newspapers to tobacco, and a cacophony of languages made it impossible to pick out any distinct conversations. I walked east, following the flow of the Thames, the river that had become my North Star in orienting myself in London. The dark and murky water looked foreboding, as though it had secrets buried far beneath its surface. I wished I could just take Violet and leave this city. I could keep her safe for now, but how long would that last? All I could think of was the look of terror on Violet's face, her small voice, the strength she had to leave her family in Ireland to follow her dream. She had a courageous streak that Rosalyn hadn't, but her youthful innocence made me nostalgic for the time when I was her age. It was my fault she had lost her room and board and I wanted to protect her in any way I could.

People are our downfall. Interacting with them is what undoes us. Your heart is too soft. It had been something Lexi told me many times over the years. I'd always nod, but sometimes I'd question why. Because while it was easy enough to avoid humans when I was in the company of Lexi, I seemed to instinctively seek out their company when I was by myself. And why was that so wrong? Just because I was a monster didn't mean that I no longer valued companionship.

So when will my heart harden? I'd asked, impatient.

She'd laughed. *I hope it won't. It's the part of you that keeps you human. I suppose that's your blessing and your curse.*

As I walked to Whitechapel, I stopped midway in St. James Park, my thirst growing. I knew if I was heading back to the tavern, I would have to be at my strongest. Unlike the nightmarish Dutfield Park from last night, this field was sprawling and lush, full of ponds and trees and pedestrians enjoying impromptu picnics. It was vast; but at first glance still seemed smaller than Central Park in New York City, where I'd once spent several hungry weeks foraging for food.

Clouds had once again rolled into the sky, bathing the

whole city in darkness. It was only noon, but there was no sign of the sun. The air felt wet and heavy with rain, despite the lack of actual drops. It was never like this in Ivinghoe. The weather there seemed more honest, somehow. When it looked like it would rain, it rained. Here, nothing was as it seemed.

I sniffed the air. Even though I couldn't see them, I knew animals were everywhere, hiding under the brush or scampering in tunnels just beneath the grass. I headed toward a dense collection of trees, hoping I could capture a bird or a squirrel without anyone noticing.

A disturbance in the bushes caused me to stiffen. Without thinking, I used my vampire reflexes to reach into them, trapping a fat gray squirrel in my hands. Relying only on instinct, I sunk my teeth into the tiny creature's neck and sucked out its blood, trying not to gag. City squirrels tasted different than country squirrels, and this one had watery, bitter-tasting blood. Still, it would have to do.

I threw the carcass into the bushes and wiped my mouth. Suddenly, I heard a rustle coming from the far end of the forest. I whirled around, half-expecting to see Klaus, ready for a fight. Nothing.

I sighed, my stomach finally quieting now that it was satiated.

And now that I was prepared, I headed to the Ten Bells

Tavern, ready to compel Alfred into giving Violet her job back. As expected, the air smelled musty and sharp, like the scent of ale mixed with unwashed human bodies.

"Alfred?" I called, my eyes once again adjusting to the near nighttime blackness of the bar. I wasn't looking forward to speaking to him. He was loathsome, and even though my compelling would ensure Violet would be treated kindly, I hated the thought of her returning here. But I knew it was the best thing for her. Because the more she became involved with me, the more danger she'd be in. That was something I knew as clearly as the message written in blood on the wall.

"Alfred?" I called again, just as he emerged from the kitchen, wiping his hands on his pants. His cheeks were red and his eyes were bloodshot.

"Stefan. Violet's bloke. I s'pose now you decided you're done with her? We don't do refunds," he said flatly, leaning his meaty arms against the bar.

"She's a friend," I said. I stepped toward him, making sure to keep eye contact, and keeping my fingers and palms flexed to avoid lashing out. I hated him. "And I have something I need to discuss."

"What?" he asked suspiciously.

"Take Violet back," I said levelly. "She's a hard worker, and she needs her job and room."

Alfred nodded, but didn't open his mouth to speak.

"Just like her sister. Takes off with the first man who looks at her nicely. Bloody fools if you ask me. Mary Ann, now she was in the wrong place at the wrong time, but Violet . . ."

"Will you do that?" I prompted. I wanted to follow his conversational thread, but I couldn't stop in the middle of compelling. In the past twenty-four hours, I'd compelled more than I had in the past twenty years, and I wasn't as confident in my Power as I used to be. "And when you do, you won't lay a hand on her. You'll protect her. Just bring Violet back."

"Bring Violet back," he said slowly, as if in a trance.

"Yes," I said, relieved by the confirmation.

Just then, the bell of the tavern tinkled and a large man lurched in, clearly still drunk from the night before. Alfred looked up at the commotion, breaking the spell and ruining my chance to ask questions: What man had Cora gone off with? And what else did Alfred know?

"You'll see Violet tomorrow night," I said to Alfred's retreating back, as though we were just having a chat. I pulled up a stool to the bar, waiting for when he'd be free. The door opened again and a woman sauntered in, wearing an indigo dress that clearly showed the expansive whiteness of her bosom. I recognized her as the woman who'd come up to me last night. This time, I was glad to speak with her. She had a large beauty mark above her

red-painted lips, and her hair hung in bright blond ring-
lets under a black-feather-adorned hat. She was short and
squat, but carried herself with the confidence of a woman
far more beautiful.

Immediately, her beady eyes locked on mine. "Hello,
there," she said, walking unsteadily up to me. "Me name's
Eliza." She held out her hand for me to kiss.

I recoiled. Even though I'd just fed, the thin squirrel blood was not enough to satisfy my deeper thirst, and
her exposed flesh was almost more than I could bear. I
could smell her blood and could almost imagine its rich,
sugar-sweet flavor coating my tongue. I pressed my lips
together and stared at the dusty cracks between the floorboards.

"I tried to talk to you last night," she continued, allowing her hand to flutter to my shoulder as though dusting
off an imaginary speck of lint. "But you only had eyes
for that girl. I thought she was so lucky, speaking with a
handsome young lad like you. I hope you enjoyed her,"
she leered.

"I *didn't*." I stepped away, hating her insinuation.
"Violet is just a friend," I said coldly.

"Well, do you need someone who's more than a friend?"
she asked, batting her dark eyelashes.

"No! I need to know . . ." I glanced toward Alfred,
but he was far down at the other end of the bar, busy

playing a game of dice with the drunk man. Still, I lowered my voice. "I need to know more about the murderer."

"You one of them coppers?" she asked suspiciously. "Because I told 'em before, I don't do discounts and I don't give out information on me friends neither. Not for all the gin in China."

I shook my head at her mangled expression. "I'm just concerned. Especially now. Apparently another woman is missing. Do you know Cora? She works here." For Violet's sake, I only hoped that Cora was alive.

"Cora?" The woman's face transformed into a grimace. "Why, she was the barmaid, right? Always thought she was so uppity and better than us, but Lord knows she was doing the same thing we was. Seems like she was just waiting for the right price," the woman said indignantly.

"Do you mean she left with a man?" I asked urgently. It was clear that this woman had been keeping a very close eye on Cora, and I hoped that would translate into a clue as to her whereabouts.

The woman nodded. "The same man who I'd been trying all night to be sweet on me. He was handsome. Said he was a producer or an actor at the Gaiety. One of them theater types. Funny sounding, though. A bit like you," she added uncertainly.

"He had an accent?" I asked, unable to contain my excitement. I didn't want to jump to conclusions, but I doubted there were many frequenters of the Ten Bells who had a Southern drawl like mine. Maybe Damon had been here. And maybe, just maybe, he knew I was in town. Maybe that was why the message had been written on the wall. It hadn't been Klaus at all, only one of Damon's stupid traps to lure me into a cat-and-mouse chase.

"You got me going all hoarse. If we're going to talk any more, you've got to get me a drink," Eliza said, yanking me from my reverie. "Double gin, please," she said, her eyes gleaming greedily.

"Of course," I said. I went to the bar and came back with a gin and a whiskey. I licked my lips as I watched Eliza take a swig. I took a careful sip of my own drink. Although I didn't want to get drunk, alcohol occasionally tempered my cravings for blood. I hoped it would this time. I needed something to distract me from Eliza's neck. I took another large gulp of whiskey.

"There, that's better. Nothing beats a spot of gin in the afternoon, don't you agree, love?" she asked, already appearing in a much better mood.

"Well, he was talkin' funny. Not like he bothered to say much to me," she added darkly. "He talked to her all night. I walked by a couple times. Said he'd bring her to the theater, show her around. Maybe get her an audition. Men say whatever pops in their heads to get a woman to go to bed," Eliza said in disgust.

"Do you remember his name? Did he have any distinctive features? Was he intimidating her?" I asked, barraging her with questions as dread rippled through my stomach.

"I don't know! Like I said, he didn't even want to talk to me!" she said indignantly. "And I s'pose it's a good thing, especially with them murders going on. Maybe it's best we stick with the blokes we know, even if they stiff us for our money when they can't . . ." She broke off and glanced at me, her eyes challenging me to get her salty innuendo.

"But what did he look like?" I asked, barely listening to what she was saying.

Her eyes cut toward me suspiciously. "Oh, you're still thinking about him? I don't know. Elegant. Tall. Dirty blond hair. But since Cora's body didn't show up in a ditch or nothin', they're probably just enjoying each other's company," she added darkly.

Dirty blond hair? I frowned. Damon's hair was dark. It was the first clue that hadn't been a perfect match. Of course, it wasn't as if Eliza was necessarily the most reliable eyewitness. I decided to keep focusing on what else she had to say. "Or maybe he really was one of those producers she always talked about. Well, la dee da for her.

Then she'd always be thinking she was better than any of us," Eliza added.

"Were you close with Mary Ann?" I asked, changing the subject to the murder victim.

Eliza sighed and flicked her gaze away from me, toward the motley collection of men who'd filled the bar since we'd begun talking. Since it was clear I wasn't interested in propositioning her, she was obviously looking for someone who would. Not seeing any targets, she glanced back at me.

"Mary Ann was me friend. At least she was before she went and got herself killed," Eliza said, a cloud of anger crossing her face. "Although, what do you expect?"

"What do you mean?" I asked.

"Well, she was me friend, and I'd'a said this to her face if I'd gotten the chance. She was one of them types. Took risks. Caroused with bad men. I don't even remember who she left with. After they found her, all cut up and killed, the police came in the tavern. Who did she go with, they asked. What did she say as she was leaving? And the answer was, we saw nothing, we heard nothing, and if she'd'a only told us who she was going off with, we might have been able to avoid him in the future!" Eliza shuddered, and I couldn't help noticing her heaving bosom. I glanced away, but not before she caught me staring.

She smiled lasciviously. "Are you sure you don't want to continue this conversation in private?" she asked, suggestively licking her lower lip.

"I'm sure!" I said forcefully, standing up so quickly the rickety chair behind me toppled over. "You're lovely, of course, but I can't," I said.

"I can give you a deal. Foreigner's special!" she said, wiggling her eyebrows.

"I have to go," I said firmly. I reached into my pocket and found a few florins. "These are for you. Please don't go off with anyone," I said. I dropped the coins into her hand.

Her eyes gleamed as she took the money. "You sure I can't give you a little something?"

"That won't be necessary." I scraped my chair back and strode out of the tavern.

As soon as I walked out, I stumbled, and immediately realized the whiskey had gone to my head. But I had a clue that would lead me to Cora and Damon.

"You there!"

I whirled around. The drunk man who'd been at the bar when I came in lurched toward me, the scent of stale gin on his breath.

"What?" I asked.

"I know who you are," he said, swaying closer and closer toward me. "And I have my eye on you!" At this, he laughed maniacally, then staggered backward against a brick wall.

Fear buzzed in my brain. I looked down at him, still laughing in a drunken heap. What did he mean, he knew who I was? Was it just the ramblings of a drunk, or was it another clue that my arrival in London hadn't been unnoticed?

I know who you are.

The words thudded in my consciousness. Who was I? I was Stefan Salvatore once. Damon knew that. So did whoever wrote the message on the wall. But who else?

He was a drunk. Let it go, I commanded myself as I hastily picked my way out of the park and toward the hotel, stopping along the way to purchase tickets for a musical burlesque at the Gaiety Theatre. I'd gotten two box tickets, each one costing more than a week's pay. But I'd compelled them from the bewildered man at the box office, justifying it by reminding myself it would all be worth it if the play led to us finding Cora. With the tickets in my breast pocket, I whistled to myself as I headed back into the hotel.

Violet jumped up as soon as I opened the door.

"How was your day?" she asked, sounding anxious and tired. "Did you find Cora?"

"I spoke to Alfred, and you don't have to worry about your job. And I think I know where we can find Cora," I said slowly, belying my own excitement. The last thing I wanted to do was give Violet false hope.

"Really? Where? How?" Violet clapped her hands together. "Oh, Stefan, you're wonderful!"

"I'm not," I said gruffly. "And I don't know for a fact, but I think she might have met a producer from the Gaiety Theatre." I briefly explained my conversation with Eliza, although I left out the part about the man with the accent. But in Violet's mind, Cora was as good as found.

"Really?" Violet beamed. "Why, no wonder she wouldn't have said anything! Because, see, Alfred would have gotten jealous. And if he'd known she'd left her job, he wouldn't allow her back. So maybe Cora was just waiting until she got the theater job before she came to collect me. That makes sense, doesn't it?"

"I suppose so," I said slowly. Violet's cheeks were red and she was striding back and forth across the room. She was excited and agitated, and I wanted to believe the story she'd spun. It could be true. But no good could come of us both pacing like caged animals in the hotel room. We had a few hours before the show, and Violet was still clad in her stained pinafore from last night.

"Let's go shopping," I decided, standing up and making my way to the door.

"Really?" Violet wrinkled her nose. "Of course I want to, but I've no money . . ."

"I have a little bit saved. Please, it's the least I can do after everything that happened last night."

Violet hesitated, then nodded, accepting my help. "Thank you!" she said. "I can't wait to see Cora. She won't believe that I had my own adventure. Why, I think she might be jealous," she continued giddily. I started to relax.

After all, I could play Violet's *what if* game, too. I could pretend the drunk outside the tavern had been hallucinating and had mistaken me for his long-lost cousin. I could pretend I was a human.

And that's where the game ended. Because I wasn't, and as much as I wanted to believe it, none of the rest was true either.

"We should go before the store closes," I said awkwardly. What was I doing? Why did I care whether this girl or her sister lived or died? Stefan Pine would go back to Ivinghoe and wake up tomorrow to milk the cows. Stefan Pine would stop reading the London papers. And Stefan Pine wouldn't be taking a girl from the gutter and buying her a dress to make up for the fact that his brother was most likely drinking her sister's blood.

But I wasn't Stefan Pine. I was Stefan Salvatore, and I was in too deep to leave. Together, we strode out into the dark afternoon. I raised my hand to fetch a coach.

Immediately, a coach pulled up to us. "Where to?" a driver asked, tipping his hat.

"Where can we go to get a dress?" I asked boldly.

"I'd bring you over to Hyde Park. Harrods."

"Really?" Violet clapped her hands in delight at the mention of the name. "That's where everyone classy shops! I read about it. I've heard even Lillie Langtry goes there!"

"Let's go," I said grandly. I had no idea what Violet was saying, but all I cared about was that she seemed happy.

We took off through the streets of London. Compared to Whitechapel, this part of the city was lovely. The streets were wide, well-dressed men and women were walking arm in arm on the sidewalk, and even the pigeons seemed clean and well-behaved. Violet looked back and forth, as if unable to decide where to direct her focus.

Finally, the driver pulled up at an imposing marble building. "Here you are!"

I paused. Should I compel my way into not paying for the ride?

"Thank you!" Violet hooked her arm in mine as she hopped out of the coach. The opportunity to compel was lost and I felt through my pockets, pulling out a few shillings and handing them to the driver.

He drove away, and Violet and I stepped through the doorway into a vaulted hallway filled with the competing scents of perfume and foods. The marble floors were so polished I could see our reflection when we gazed down. Everyone spoke in a slightly raised whisper, as if we were in a church. And indeed, it seemed like a holy place.

Violet sighed in ecstasy. "It sounds like a sin, but when I was little, our priest asked us to imagine heaven. I always thought it would look like this. Everything shiny and new," she said, echoing my thoughts as we walked through the winding aisles of the department store. A section selling stationery gave way to one selling toys, which opened into a massive food hall. It was as if anything anyone could imagine was under one roof.

Finally, we reached the back of the store. Dresses of all colors were hanging on racks, and women were milling around the displays as if they were at a cocktail party. Saleswomen were standing behind glass cases, ready to help customers.

"You can have anything you want," I said, splaying my hands as if to show her the extent of the wares.

But Violet seemed sad. "I wish Cora were here. She would love it."

"We'll find Cora," I said firmly.

"May I help you?" a woman in a dark black dress asked, gliding up to us.

"We need a gown," I said, nodding toward Violet.

"Of course," the woman said. She gave Violet a glance from head to toe, but refrained from saying anything about her shabby clothes. Instead, she smiled.

"We have some things that will do very well. Come with me," she said, motioning for Violet to join her.

She turned toward me. "You stay here. When I'm through with her, you won't even recognize her."

For a second, I paused. I didn't want to let Violet out of my sight. Then I laughed to myself. I was being paranoid. We were in the finest department store in the world. It wasn't as if the saleswoman would hurt her.

"All right, then?" The saleswoman arched her black eyebrow as if sensing my discomfort.

"Of course," I said. I settled onto a plush peach-colored settee and glanced around. I felt like Whitechapel was in a different country. Could it be possible just to stay on this side of the town and forget about the murderer? I wanted to, badly.

"Stefan?"

I glanced up and gasped. Violet was clad in an emerald-green dress that accentuated her small waist and red hair. Even though her face was still drawn and there were dark shadows under her large eyes, she looked beautiful.

"What do you think?" she asked shyly, twirling in the mirror.

"She's lovely, isn't she?" the saleswoman murmured.

"We tried two others as well, and your wife looks equally exquisite in all of them."

"She's not . . . yes," I said simply. It was so much easier to lie. "We'll take this dress. We'll take all of them," I said, pulling her aside to compel her to give us the purchases for free. The expression in Violet's eyes was worth it.

Instead of taking a coach back to the hotel, we walked. Every so often, I caught her stealing glances of herself in the windows, twisting the skirts of her new emerald-green dress. It was nice that I could make someone happy.

"I fear I won't be able to repay you," Violet said at one point.

"No need." I shook my head. "Your friendship is repayment enough."

"Thank you. But I feel like I'm not being a good friend. All I do is talk about myself. I only know your name, and that you're from America. Are you a businessman?"

I laughed. "No, I work on a farm. I'm just like you. And I know what it's like to lose a family member. My brother once went missing. I was worried sick about him."

"Did he turn up?" she asked, her eyes wide.

"Eventually. And I know you'll see Cora soon." My heart went out to Violet and her missing sister. "Tell me more about her," I said.

"Well, we fought of course. But all siblings do, don't they? She had to do everything first. And of course I wanted to be just like her. I don't think that I would have moved to London without her. And now that she's not here . . ."

"You have to figure out who you are," I murmured.

"Yes," Violet agreed. "But it's hard to know who I am without Cora. We're that close. Is that what it's like with you and your brother?

"No." I shook my head.

"Did you have a falling-out?"

"Yes, but that's long in the past. Right now, I'm only focused on my future," I said, offering the crook of my elbow for her to loop her arm through.

"Well, your brother's making a mistake, to fight with you," she said.

"And I'd never fight with you, if you were my sister," I said. I was enjoying our comfortable back-and-forth.

We stopped by the hotel to drop off our bags with the bellhop and then continued on our way to the theater.

"I feel like this is a dream and I don't want to wake up," Violet said, her eyes shining as an usher led us to our seats. Being with Violet felt natural, and our easy banter reminded me of the way that Damon, I, and the rest of the boys would tease the Mystic Falls girls at barbecues and social functions during the year.

Suddenly, the theater went dark and the curtain rose on the stage.

"Oh, Stefan!" Violet said, clapping her hands together as she perched on the very edge of the velvet-covered chair and leaned her elbows on the railing of the box. Dozens of chorus girls came out, wearing flouncy skirts and large hats, and I tried to pay attention to the song they were singing. But I couldn't. All I could think of was Damon. Why had he done this? It had taken years, but I'd found peace. Couldn't he do the same? He could feed on women and have his fancy parties all he liked. I just wanted him to stop destroying other people's lives. I was convinced that we could both live and let live. But I couldn't live if my brother was killing.

I saw Violet glance at me and I tried to look as if I were enjoying the show. But inside, I was frustrated. I hated the way everything *always* came back to Damon, and most likely would, for eternity.

"I didn't see Cora," Violet said in disappointment. "Maybe she's not in this show."

"Hmmm?" I asked, realizing the curtain had gone down and thunderous applause was emanating from all corners of the theater house.

"The show! The first act is over," Violet said. "And, oh, Stefan, it was ever so lovely!"

"You liked it, then?" I asked mechanically. If Cora wasn't here, had we just wasted another night? Maybe the Journeyman was still open. I was about to tell Violet our plan when I noticed tears leaking from the corner of her eyes.

"If only . . ." she began.

"If only what?" I asked.

"If only Cora were here. Every time the curtain opened, I'd just cross my fingers and send a prayer to St. Jude, but . . . oh well. I still liked the show. Thank you," she said, smiling wistfully.

"I understand," I said, squeezing her hand. I did understand. When Damon had gone away to fight in the Civil War, back when we were humans, I'd always felt a half second of regret whenever I was doing anything enjoyable, thinking how much better it would have been if only he'd been there to be part of it. And even though I knew beyond a shadow of a doubt I was now better off without my brother, there was still a vestigial pull that wished I could be with him. The more I saw of the world, the more I realized that not all people had bonds like mine with their siblings. And maybe that was far better than what I'd had, and what I'd lost.

The curtain opened again and another act, more opulent than the last, began. I tried to watch, but I couldn't keep track of something even so elementary as who played the lover or the villain, and the lyrics for the musical numbers seemed silly, not charming. So I watched Violet instead. Lit up in the glow of the stage lights, she looked absolutely entranced, and the happiest I'd ever seen her in our short time of knowing each other.

As the curtain came down, I stood and clapped politely along with the audience.

"Oh, Stefan, thank you!" Violet said, spontaneously throwing her arms around me. "I don't want this night to end!"

"You're welcome," I said, shifting my weight from side to side impatiently. In front of us, the lead actress stood on stage, blowing kisses to the audience, while members of the front row were throwing flowers toward her.

Violet sighed theatrically, unable to tear her eyes away from the stage. "Cora should have been in that play," she said, her voice adamant with resolution. "Charlotte Dumont doesn't have anything on her."

"Who?" I asked. The name sounded familiar.

"Why, Charlotte Dumont. The actress."

"She was *here*?" I asked. Charlotte was the woman who Count DeSangue was consorting with. Maybe this hadn't been such a waste of time.

"Stef-an!" Violet said playfully. "She was the lead actress. Wasn't she wonderful?" Violet's eyes danced, but I wasn't paying attention. My eyes were scanning the crowd for my brother.

"Just once, I'd like to stand out," Violet continued, oblivious to my distraction. "Back at Ten Bells, I feel invisible. I want to feel unique. Like I did when I was little. You know, when your parents think you're special, and you believe them?" Violet said wistfully as she daintily picked up her skirts to walk down the winding stairs of the theater and onto the street. Watching her from a few steps back, I was amazed at how different she looked from the sad barmaid of last night. In her finery, she had all the confidence and airs of a woman who'd grown up in luxury.

"You are special," I said, meaning it. She was charming and fun and I knew that once she believed in herself, she'd find people who believed in her.

"Why, thank you," Violet said coquettishly. Around us, people turned to gaze at her. I was certain they were gawking because they were trying to place her—had she been one of the comic ingénues they'd just seen onstage? Violet smiled, clearly basking in the attention.

"What shall we do now?" Violet asked, her eyes shining.

We'd reached the cool street and I breathed out, glancing around. Even though it was late, the street was crowded with passersby. A few paces down, I noticed streams of people were entering the small black door marked STAGE. I made a split-second decision.

"I have an idea," I said. "We're going to meet Charlotte." I pasted a smile on my face as I marched toward the door.

"Name?" a small man with slicked-back black hair

asked, glancing at the leather-bound book clutched in his hands.

"Name?" I repeated, in mock confusion, trying to get him to look up at me.

"Yes, your name," the man said with exaggerated patience, finally glancing up at me. "I'm afraid the party is guest list only."

"Sir Stefan Pine. And my wife, Lady Violet," I added as Violet giggled delightedly beside me. Even though his job was to guard the door, the vague slurring of his words made it obvious he'd been taking in drinks as the audience members had been taking in the performance. I didn't so much have to compel him as confuse him.

"Yes, sir," he said, barely glancing back down at his list as he ushered us inside.

Violet widened her eyes, but I merely placed a finger on my lips and followed the crush of people into the cavernous backstage.

We turned into a brightly lit room that was almost as big as a ballroom, already filled with actors in various states of costume as well as audience members, whom I recognized as the well-heeled fellow members of our box. We were definitely in the right place. Now, all we had to do was find Charlotte. It was almost too easy.

And then I felt a tap on my shoulder.

I whirled around.

There, with a wide smile, thick dark hair, and an inscru-
table expression in his bright blue eyes, was Damon.

"Hello, brother," Damon said, flashing a wide grin.

I grinned back. I'd play nice. For now.

his is your brother?" Violet asked curiously, her lilting voice rising. "The one who . . ."

"No!" I waved my arm in front of me, as though batting away an absurd question. "An old friend," I lied. My heart thudded against my rib cage. Even though I'd been actively seeking him out all afternoon, it was a shock to be face-to-face again after all these years.

"Oh yes, Stefan and I go way back." Damon leered. "In fact, sometimes I think I'd die for him."

I shifted uneasily, appraising my brother, all too aware of Violet standing next to me. I studied him, taking in each aspect of his appearance.

He hadn't aged. It was a ludicrous observation, but it was the first one that struck me. Of course, I hadn't either, but I was so used to seeing my face in the glass every

morning that it wasn't remarkable, just a fact of my existence. But seeing Damon as fresh-faced and wrinkle-free
as he'd been the night we'd both died was jarring.

But, on closer inspection, there was a difference. His
eyes had changed. They seemed darker, somehow, full of
secrets and horrors and deaths. Who knew what he'd done
these past twenty years? If it was anything like what he'd
been doing in London, then he'd been keeping himself
and local law enforcement agencies quite busy.

"You're looking good," Damon remarked, as if we were
neighbors who'd merely bumped into each other in a town
square, not brothers who'd last seen each other across the
ocean decades ago.

"As are you," I allowed. His dark hair was slicked back
and he was wearing an expensive suit with a silk tie knotted around his neck.

"And who's this lovely lady?" Damon asked, extending
his hand to Violet.

"She's none of your concern—"

"I'm Violet Burns," Violet said, curtseying and blushing
as Damon took her hand and brought it to his lips for a kiss.

"Charmed. Damon DeSangue," Damon said. I grimaced at the familiar way the false name dripped off his
tongue. I did note, however, that he'd lost the affected
Italian accent he'd insisted on using back in New York.

"And what are we doing here?" he asked.

"We're just leaving—"

"No!" Violet interjected. "Please, let us stay. Our hotel is ever so close, we're right at the Cumberland," she said to Damon, batting her eyes as if to charm him. "And we're looking for my sister," she added, her voice drowned out by Damon's showy display of shock at our choice of hotel.

"The Cumberland!" Damon said as my stomach sank. The last thing I wanted was for him to know the name of our hotel. "Aren't you moving up in the world, Stefan!"

No more games, I said under my breath. *We're too old for that.*

I never outgrew my fondness for games, Damon replied, not moving his lips.

Just don't hurt her, I said through gritted teeth. But Damon didn't say anything, and only half-shook his head in a gesture that was impossible for me to read. Violet continued to stare at him, her expression worshipful. Typical. Damon always commanded attention from women. Just then, a tall, beautiful woman wearing a midnight-blue silk dress and false eyelashes swanned up to him, two glasses of champagne in her hands. I spotted a gold-threaded silk scarf wrapped several times around her neck. I was sure if she unwrapped it, I'd see two small puncture holes on her neck from Damon's fangs. Damon, noticing my gaze, raised his eyebrow and smirked. Violet let out a gasp.

"Charlotte Dumont!" she squealed, clapping her hands with delight. I smiled at her, happy she'd at least been paying attention to the show. I couldn't believe I'd let such an obvious clue almost slip through my fingers.

"Why, yes, that's my name," Charlotte said, giggling as she handed a champagne flute to Damon. "I can't leave you for a moment!" she said to Damon, playfully swatting him on his arm. "Every time I do, I come back to see a crowd fawning over you. And I'm supposed to be the star of our twosome!" She pouted.

"Don't worry, darling," Damon said, placing his hand on her shoulder in a move so tender, it surprised me. Did he actually like this woman, or was he just using her for money and status? "This is my old friend, Stefan . . . if that's what you're going by nowadays?"

"Stefan Pine, and this is my friend, Violet," I explained, taking Charlotte's delicate hand and bringing it to my lips for a kiss.

"I'm an actress. From America," Violet said, trying hard to put on an American accent as she sank into a deep curtsy.

"Are you?" Charlotte asked pointedly, a sharp edge to her tone as she tried to determine whether or not Violet was competition.

"Well, I'd like to be," Violet demurred, clearly realizing that her statement was not the best way to get in

Charlotte's good graces. "So would my sister. Cora Burns. Do you know her?"

Charlotte's expression softened slightly. "Cora . . . the name sounds familiar," Charlotte said, tugging on Damon's shirtsleeve. "Do we know a Cora, love?"

Damon rolled his eyes. "As if I could keep track of everyone we meet. That's what the society pages are for, right? If they're there, then I've met them. And if not, then I haven't."

"Well, if you meet her, please tell her that her sister is looking for her," Violet said tentatively. I felt nothing but relief. Charlotte seemed somewhat familiar with Cora's name. Maybe Cora simply had gone off with a theater producer.

"Doesn't ring a bell, sweetheart, sorry." Damon shrugged.

"It's okay," Violet said sadly. "Just so she knows I'm looking."

"Speaking of looking," Charlotte said brightly, breaking the silence, "I think I need another glass of champagne." In the short conversation, she'd already drained her whole flute. "Would you like to come with me? And maybe if you're lucky, I'll introduce you to Mr. Mackintosh, the producer of our little show. Your sister's not the only one who could be an actress."

Violet's eyes gleamed as the two girls walked away

into the swirl of revelers. Damon watched with a bemused expression.

"Women!" he remarked once they were firmly out of earshot. "Can't live with them, can't live without them. Am I right? The nagging, the compliments, the enthusiasm . . . no wonder humans age so quickly," he said, throwing back his own glass of champagne.

"Well, it seems you have a steady source of nourishment," I said darkly. Was Damon's choice of women what ignited the wrath of Klaus? Or something else? Whatever it was, I'd play nice until I got to the bottom of it.

"Oh yes. She does well, although the blood is often rather alcoholic. Great before a big night out, but I have to be careful not to overindulge," Damon said casually, as if he were reviewing a brand-new restaurant. "And you? Have you gone back to human blood in your middle age? Don't tell me you're still subsisting on squirrels and bunnies!" He guffawed.

"I'm not talking about Charlotte," I said, ignoring his teasing. "And I'm here to stop you. You're being stupid and careless, and you're going to get hurt. What are you even doing here?"

"I'm here for the weather," Damon parried back sarcastically. "Do I need a reason? Maybe I decided to see the sights. America felt too small. Here, there are all sorts of diversions."

"What kind of diversions?" I asked pointedly.

Damon smiled again, revealing his ultra-white teeth. "You know, the usual ones that come with traveling abroad: meeting new people, trying new cuisines . . ."

"Trying your hand at murder?" I hissed, lowering my voice so that no one else could hear me.

Confusion crossed Damon's face, followed by a long, hollow laugh.

"Oh, you mean the Jack the Ripper nonsense? Please. Don't you know me better?" Damon asked when he finally stopped chuckling.

"I know you well enough," I said, clenching my jaw. "And I know you love attention. This is bad news for you."

"No news is bad news for me." Damon yawned, as if the conversation bored him. "Well, then you know, *brother*, that I've always abhorred guessing games and I have no patience for hysteria. I'd much rather kill discreetly."

"So you haven't killed anyone recently?" I asked, my eyes darting around the room to make sure no one was listening. No one was. The partiers around us were far too busy drinking and laughing to think anything of our intense conversation in the shadows.

"No!" Damon said, annoyed. "I'm having far too much fun with my wicked lady of the stage. And let me tell you, she is wicked," he said, suggestively waggling his eyebrows.

"Fine," I said. I wouldn't give Damon the satisfaction of listening to his exploits. "But the murders . . ."

"Are being done by some stupid human who'll be caught sooner or later," Damon said, shrugging.

"No." I shook my head and briefly explained what I'd seen, the bloody SALVATORE—I SHALL HAVE MY REVENGE message in Dutfield Park.

"So?" Damon asked, barely a flicker crossing his face.

"I think it could be Klaus," I snapped, frustrated at having to spell out what appeared so obvious to me. "Who else writes bloody messages and knows our name?"

Damon's eyes widened slightly, only to immediately go back to his satisfied, lazy expression. "That's your clue?" he asked. "Because anyone could write that. And I hate to bruise your ego, Stefan, but we're not exactly the only Salvatores in the world. It could even be the name of one of those Whitechapel girls. I'm not concerned. And of course the murderer, whoever he was, used blood to write. Ink and paper just doesn't have the same horrific effect." He sighed, glancing over to the bar, where Violet and Charlotte were tipping back their glasses of champagne and giggling.

"Now, if you'll excuse me, I need a drink. Come with me, brother. Let's celebrate our reunion," he said, picking his way through the crowd. I followed him, furious. He was acting like I'd told him a joke. Didn't he care that a psychotic vampire was on the loose? Didn't it bother him that we might be the target of a murderer?

Apparently not. Every few steps, he was stopped by various admirers: girls I recognized from the chorus, a small man with an enormous white bushy beard who seemed to be the theater tailor, and a barrel-chested man with gold cufflinks and a top hat whom I imagined to be one of the producers for the company. I tried to ask him light questions to see if he had any connection to Cora, but I knew this man wasn't the one. He had a thick British accent and dark hair. Nothing like Eliza's description. Every time Damon was stopped, he laughed and smiled, clinking his glass and offering up compliments. I had to hand it to him—on the surface, Damon was nothing but a perfect gentleman.

"See how well I'm behaving?" Damon asked after we finally got to the bar and the bartender offered us two glasses of champagne.

"Like a regular priest," I said. It was odd to be at a party with Damon. One part of me still wanted it to be like it had been back when we were humans, when we'd always anticipate what the other was going to do or say. The other, wiser part of me knew I could never trust Damon as a vampire—after all, he'd killed Callie, he'd have killed the Sutherlands if Klaus and his minions hadn't gotten to them first, and he left Lexi and I twenty years ago, barely saying good-bye.

And yet, in his mind, nothing would settle the score that Damon thought existed between us. After all, I was the one who'd turned Damon into a vampire. He'd begged me not to, but I'd forced him to drink blood, had forced him to live out this eternity. He'd never forgiven me. Over time, even though there was a mounting list of offenses and wrongs that he'd done me, I still would erase them all from my mind if it meant we could be true brothers, like we'd been before. And it was all too painful to realize that would never come to pass when, even to outsiders, we appeared to be the best of friends. Indeed, Damon was constantly introducing me to a whole host of people as his "old friend Stefan from the States," and all I could do was smile, nod, and wish I lived in a world where it truly was that simple.

"Charlotte was bewitching as always," I heard a voice say and glanced up. A tall blond gentleman was standing next to Damon. He was wearing a white silk shirt buttoned all the way to the top of his neck, along with an elegant black topcoat. His shoes were Italian leather, and it was impossible to tell his age—he could be anywhere from twenty-five to forty.

"Samuel!" Damon exclaimed, giving the man a hearty clap on the back. "This is Stefan, an old friend."

"Hello," I said stiffly, bowing my head slightly. I sensed Samuel appraising my rough hands, chapped and cut up from weeks of hard physical labor, as well as the five o'clock shadow forming on my face. I'd fallen out of the habit of daily shaves while at Abbott Manor.

"Welcome," Samuel said after a long moment. "Any friend of Damon's is a friend of mine." But before he could say anything else, Charlotte and Violet walked toward us, Violet clearly tipsy.

"This is the most exquisite day of my life!" Violet announced to no one in particular, flinging her champagne glass up in a toast so violently that the liquid sprayed in a constellation-like pattern on her silk dress.

"To imagine, I was like that once," Charlotte said in mock horror. "I do hope you take her home and teach her some of the finer points of mingling in polite society," she added, looking pointedly at me.

"Well, unfortunately, Violet will get none of that with Stefan, darling. Although she will get a lot of lessons. Stefan loves hearing himself talk. Why, I think he's talked me to death in the past."

"I almost love talking as much as Damon loves listening to himself," I said, an undercurrent of annoyance evident beneath my jocular tone. I needed to get Violet back to the hotel. After all, she had to work tomorrow night. But I knew it would be a challenge to get her to willingly leave this party. And we still hadn't found Cora.

"Well, I must go, but will I see you and Charlotte tomorrow near Grove House?" Samuel asked after a moment, glancing meaningfully at Damon.

"Of course." Damon nodded.

"One o'clock? It has to be before my show," Charlotte said.

"Yes," Samuel said. "And, Stefan? Would you and your friend like to come? It could be amusing," he said dryly. I blinked at him. I felt everything he said was just on the edge of an insult, but it was impossible to pinpoint what was so offensive about the words themselves.

"Want to come to a party, brother?" Damon asked, raising his eyebrows.

"Oh, please?" Violet asked, clapping her hands together.

"We'll see," I said stiffly.

"Violet, would you like to come?" Typical Damon. "Stefan will if he can pencil it in between his moralizing, Shakespeare reading, and detective work."

"Detective work?" Charlotte asked in confusion.

"Never mind, pet," Damon said. "Inside joke."

"It's a boring story," I said. "Far more interesting is Damon's love of drama. You should get him to talk about the acts he's pulled off."

"You're an actor?" Violet asked.

"We'll talk more at the party!" Damon said, clearly

annoyed. Well, good. If talking in code and getting under his skin was the way to get him to pay attention to me, then I'd do it.

"Yes!" Violet said eagerly.

"We should probably be going," I said gently, taking Violet's arm and escorting her through the throngs of people and out the door.

I breathed a sigh of relief as the cool air hit my face. It was the perfect antidote to the hot, crowded, tense atmosphere of the party. I didn't think about Damon. I focused on the buzz of the gas lamps above and the flutter of the leaves and the staccato steps of pedestrians—all of the everyday noises I heard, amplified because of my senses, but rarely appreciated.

Once we got back to the room, I placed Violet on the bed, gently tucking the coverlet around her body. Her eyes were fully shut by the time her head hit the silk pillowcase.

I took longer to fall asleep. Outside, the streets of London were still buzzing, and every time I closed my eyes, I thought I could hear Damon's laugh, wafting up from the streets and into my mind.

9

𝕴've always been a brother. It's a thought that comes to me, unbidden, late at night or when I'm walking silently through the forest, stalking my prey. No matter who knows that about me, or whether or not I share that information, it's a part of me that I can never forget.

When I came along, of course, I had my parents, but they were older, authoritarian, a presence in the morning and in the evening. But Damon was always by my side. He was who I explored the world with, who I rebelled against, who I occasionally yearned to be.

On the other hand, Damon was not always a brother. As the eldest, there were years where it was just him, alone in the world. He'd never had *the constant sense that he was being compared to someone else. He'd never known what it was like to always be reaching for the sun while standing in the shadow of another.*

I don't think he ever felt that way about me. He was always the older brother, always showing me how things were done, always coaxing me to ride a horse I was frightened of, or kiss a girl whom I was worried wouldn't like me back. I watched him, wide-eyed, as he conquered the world.

And even now, I couldn't break free from him. I couldn't stop being a younger brother, who was simultaneously fearful and in awe of the unique force that was Damon Salvatore.

"How do I look?" I woke to Violet prancing into the room, wearing a light blue dress with a crinoline underneath that rustled with every step.

"You look lovely," I said as I sat up and stretched my arms over my head. I couldn't believe I had allowed myself to sleep past dawn; usually I was wide awake well before the sun rose. But despite all my troubled thoughts, the comfortable couch had lulled me into a deep, dreamless sleep.

I wondered what was happening at the Abbott Manor, who was taking care of the chickens and livestock.

I imagined Oliver glancing out the window, waiting for me to come home to take him hunting. It was a world away.

"What time do you think we should leave?" Violet asked.

"For what?" I asked, deliberately playing dumb. I hoped that Damon's mention of the afternoon party had been washed from Violet's memory by the rivers of champagne she'd consumed last night.

"Why, for the party your friend invited us to attend. We *are* going, aren't we? It sounds like fun. Plus, Charlotte mentioned her producer will be there, who couldn't be there last night. Maybe he's the man who met with Cora," she said, smoothing invisible folds of her dress with her small hands. Violet was definitely priming herself to be a woman like Charlotte, with a slew of eager men ready to do her bidding and compliment her at any moment. And even though Violet's preening should have been exasperating, she was so wide-eyed and enthusiastic, like a child playing dress-up, that it was nothing more than adorable. "Are you sure I look all right? I wouldn't want them to think I was a slattern from the slums. After all, I told them that I was an actress from America. From Cal-*eye*-forn-ia," she said, overemphasizing the second syllable.

"California," I corrected. "And your accent sounds grand." It was funny. The longer Violet and I spent together, the more we seemed to adopt each other's accents. She did sound half-convincing as an American, although I was sure that I sounded positively ridiculous using a vague Irish brogue.

Violet nodded. "How do you know Damon again? He kept calling you brother. Is it something all people in America say?" she asked, furrowing her eyebrows. I knew if I answered yes, she'd add that phrase to her repertoire. She'd asked me that last night as well, as I was half-escorting, half-carrying her up the stairs, but I hadn't answered.

"No, most people don't call each other that unless they're blood relations, but it's something Damon's been calling me ever since I can remember. It's quite a long and boring story, really," I lied. "I've known Damon forever, through the good and the bad. I know he's charming, but don't let him fool you. He's sometimes not what he appears." I said the last part semicasually, as if I was mentioning something only somewhat scandalous, like a fondness for drink or a notorious family. I only hoped she'd take my warning seriously.

"I'm sure," she said, giving herself one final glance in the looking glass. "He seems like one of those men whom all women fall over. You'll be pleased to know that I am not typical."

"You're not just saying that so I feel better about going to the party, are you?" I asked, trying to reclaim the teasing tone we'd had yesterday. But something was off.

"I just thought it would be fun," Violet said, turning toward me and biting her lip.

"You're right," I decided. Whether I liked it or not, Damon was in London. And until I was absolutely certain Klaus wasn't here for revenge, then I wouldn't be able to get him out of my head.

"Thank you . . . brother!" Violet exclaimed, kissing me on the cheek.

"Of course," I murmured. We were just going to a picnic. It would be broad daylight. Violet had the vervain, gleaming at the hollow of her throat. Nothing could happen, right?

An hour later, Violet and I were traipsing through the manicured lawns of Regent's Park. I had pulled a sheet from the bed and was holding it over my arm as an improvised blanket. My stomach was growling yet again. Violet glanced at me funnily, and I wondered if she'd heard it too. I coughed to mask the sound.

The park was dotted with children playing, kites flying, and several large mansions rising from the green lawns like oversized statues. I glanced at the sun. We were supposed to go to Grove House, which the front desk porter at the hotel had told me was at the eastern end of the park.

"There they are!" Violet exclaimed, racing across the

park, her auburn hair flying behind her.

I slowly followed her. Ahead of me was an enormous limestone structure with Grecian columns. The lawn held several tables covered with white linen. I dropped my sheet on the ground. This wasn't a picnic; this seemed to be a feast. And vampire or not, I'd been acting like a country bumpkin by toting the oversized sheet along with me, as if this were one of the church socials that Damon and I used to attend as boys.

By the time I walked over, Violet was already sipping a glass of champagne as she gestured animatedly to Damon. She was trying too hard to do her American accent, pronouncing my name as *Stef-ain*, and even trying to coax a *y'all* out of her Irish brogue, even though I'd told her multiple times on the way over that wasn't a common phrase in the American lexicon at large.

"Brother, welcome," Damon said grandly, as if he were inviting me to his private home. For all I knew, he was.

"Are you living here now?" I asked, glancing at the building, which seemed even bigger than some of the museums I'd seen back in New York City.

"No," Damon scoffed. "He is," he said, gesturing to the slight, cream-suited, ginger-haired man standing next to him.

"Lord Ainsley," the man said, offering his hand.

"Hello," I said, still amazed at the vastness of the house.

It was clear Damon was traveling in an incredibly power-ful circle. Compared to Damon's friends, George Abbott would seem like a little boy playing make-believe.

"This is an old friend from the States, Stefan Salvatore," Damon said quickly. I stiffened. Hadn't he heard me last night introducing myself as Stefan Pine? I didn't want to drag the Salvatore name into any business relating to my nature, especially not now. I knew that no one would know the Salvatore story—it was a minor footnote even in our home state of Virginia—but I still wanted to protect the name—and myself—whenever I could.

"Stefan, it's nice to meet you. Are you a steel man? Railroad?" Lord Ainsley asked, giving me a once-over.

"Um . . ." It was a good question. Who was Stefan Salvatore? I gave a pointed look in my brother's direction, eager to hear what he'd come up with.

"He has a farm back in the States," Damon interjected. "He's visiting here. Imagine my luck when I ran into him last night at the Gaiety party."

"A farm," Lord Ainsley said, instantly losing interest. "And how long will you stay in our fair city?"

"That depends," I said, locking eyes with Damon. But before he could say anything, Samuel sidled up to us, a glass of lemonade in his hands.

"Hello," he said, his voice welcoming. "I see you weren't turned off by us degenerates. Late-night parties, lots of champagne . . . that's why I'm glad Lord Ainsley had this picnic. It's refreshing to not always be a creature of the night. Isn't that what you always say, Damon?"

"I do indeed," Damon said, smirking at me. I fumed silently. Everything about Damon, from his waistcoat to the top hat he insisted on wearing to his affected European accent, annoyed me. Damon seemed determined to prove he was above everything—even bloody attacks that seemed to be committed solely as a warning toward him. Didn't he remember what Klaus had done to us back in New York? Didn't he care? Or was he simply going to distract himself with sandwiches and champagne, society gossip and women, until it was far too late?

"And, Stefan?" Samuel asked, staring down his aquiline nose to peer at me. "What did you think of the party? I imagine it's a change from . . . wherever you came from," he said, barely concealing a snicker.

"Yes, we enjoyed the party. Violet was especially taken by it," I said, forcing a smile.

"And are you taken by the young Violet?" Samuel asked curiously, setting his empty crystal glass on one of the white tables. Almost instantly, the empty one was whisked away by a white-suited butler. It could be easy to get used to this lifestyle. But I knew from experience that this type of existence always came with a price.

"Violet's taken by the stage," I explained. "I have no

interest in her, other than as a friend. I only want to make sure she's safe."

"You only want to make sure she's safe," Samuel repeated. Was there a slight trace of mockery in his tone or was I imagining it? "That's very noble of you."

"Ever since I've known him, Stefan can't resist playing the hero to a damsel in distress," Damon said languorously. I shot him a look, but he only smiled back at me. I shifted from one foot to the other and eyed him suspiciously. Here in London, it seemed everyone, and Damon especially, never said exactly what they meant.

"Well, you'll find that there's no shortage of distressed damsels in our city," Samuel said wryly. "I assume you've heard about our murderer?"

"The murderer?" I asked. I hoped it didn't sound too eager. At the horrific word, several couples turned to stare at me.

"They think he attacked again, last night. The Ripper is what all the papers call him. They think he might be a butcher, the way he cuts the bodies up." Charlotte wrinkled her nose as she strode over to us from a willow tree, where she'd been holding court in the center of a group of women. The group shuddered. Just the name—the *Ripper*—had the effect of a storm cloud over the idyllic summer day. It felt like the temperature had dropped twenty degrees.

The Ripper. I tried to catch Damon's eye, but he avoided

my gaze. He was at the party last night. Unless . . . my thoughts were whirling.

Charlotte possessively slipped her arm around Damon's waist. "I'm glad I have someone to protect me. It's so awful."

I glanced over at Violet. She was listening, rapt, the vervain charm still gleaming around her neck. *Good.*

"Who was the victim?" I asked.

"Another prostitute. No one, really." A broad-shouldered girl sniffed, as if the entire affair was far too torrid to discuss.

Samuel pulled a newspaper out of his waistcoat pocket and made a big show of opening it. "Jane's only upset because the murderer is pushing her off the page. Suddenly, all the society news has been cut for murder coverage," Samuel said, smiling sarcastically at the woman.

"What was her name?" Violet asked tremulously.

"The name of the victim? Why should that matter?" Jane shrugged derisively.

"Annie something," Samuel said, flicking through the story in the paper.

Violet's shoulders sagged in relief, and I closed my eyes in thanks. Cora was still alive. For now.

"Whatever her name is, it's quite awful, isn't it?" Lord Ainsley shuddered, joining our conversation. "Thank God he's at least picking off the East End. Once he gets to our kind, then we'll worry," he said with a loud guffaw. I shot a look at Violet, who'd sidled up to Charlotte. Her dress and mannerisms were almost indistinguishable from Charlotte's, and no one would dream that she was not one of their kind. Still, Lord Ainsley's casual flippancy about the lower class—Violet's class—made my stomach turn.

"He wrote a letter to the *Courier*," Samuel said. "Let me find it." Samuel sat down on one of the white chairs and, crossing his legs at the knee, cleared his throat and began to read.

"The return address reads 'From hell' . . ." he intoned.

The words thudded in my ears and I staggered to find a seat. I couldn't breathe. *From hell.* Maybe it was some sort of terrible prank, but I couldn't help but wonder if there was some truth to it. Was it Klaus—or someone even worse? I held on to the edge of the table for support, and I could sense Violet turn to stare at me.

"'From hell' . . . but is that a worse address than 'Whitechapel'?" Samuel snorted.

"I've never been there," a pretty, redheaded girl said as she took a large swig of champagne. "Is it as awful as everyone says?"

"Worse!" Samuel said, amid laughter. He glanced back at the paper. "Scotland Yard and the London police force have been working round the clock, but clues to the grisly murders are few and far between . . ."

I stopped listening and took a few steps away from the group. From here, the unfolding scene looked idyllic: just a group of wealthy and carefree young friends enjoying their privileges. What would they do if they knew there was a monster in their midst? And not the one they were currently laughing about?

From hell. With every clue, I was more sure that Klaus was in London. The big question was: Why didn't Damon care?

Klaus was indeed from hell—it was his legacy. The majority of us vampires had been turned at the hand of another vampire. Lexi had been turned by a lover, Damon and I had been turned by Katherine, and there were millions of other stories, just like ours, within the vampire world. But then, there were the Originals, from hell itself. They'd never experienced any years as a human. They had no humanity to temper their instincts and, as such, they were brutal and dangerous.

I shivered, even though the air was still, with no breeze rustling the elm trees above us.

"Are you all right, sir?" a butler asked, stepping up to me, holding out a plate of cucumber sandwiches.

I took one. The cucumber was slimy going down my throat and I almost gagged at the sogginess of the bread. The sandwich did nothing to quell my hunger. Of course it didn't. But at this point, the idea of blood sickened me.

I turned on my heel and went back to join the picnic, the sandwich sitting like a rock in my stomach. By the time I'd returned, the conversation had drifted to lighter fare: the unusually hot summer, the fact that no one seemed inclined to go to their country homes for the weekend anymore, and the recent establishment of secret parties down at the Canary Wharf docks.

"A word?" I asked, pulling Damon from the group and walking a distance away, toward the manicured garden that surrounded the house. The scent of roses was heady in the air, and for an instant, I was transported back to our Mystic Falls labyrinth. It had been where the two of us would teasingly fight for Katherine's favor while escorting her on afternoon walks, before we had any idea what a dangerous game we were playing.

"Yes, brother?" Damon asked, sighing impatiently. I forced myself to look into his dark eyes, nothing like the eyes of my human brother. Damon was different. I was different. It was time for me to stop thinking of the past.

A slow grin broke onto his face, and I followed his gaze to the sheet I'd tossed aside when we'd come in. "Is that yours?" Damon asked. "Aren't you fancy? That's genuine Egyptian cotton, fit for a king."

"It was for the picnic," I said. "I hadn't realized it would be so formal."

"Stealing linens from the Cumberland Hotel." Damon

shook his head. "Have you finally developed a bit of a wicked streak? That would make you almost interesting."

"And I suppose if I were you, I'd be stealing the maids from the hotel for blood, right?" I asked. "I'm concerned about the Ripper," I added. I took a bloom and snapped it from its stem, feeling the velvety softness of the rose's pink petals. Despite my wish only a second ago to forget the past, my mind flashed back to the petal-pulling *he loves me, he loves me not* game that Katherine had tortured me with.

I plucked a petal. *I trust him, I trust him not,* I thought as I dropped each silky flower fragment to the grass.

"You're concerned about the Ripper." Damon sneered. "Why? Are you a woman? Are you a whore? You know those are his victims. You're obsessed, brother! Find a woman to be obsessed with, it's more rewarding."

"Yes, I'm sure it's rewarding to run and fetch champagne at every snap of Charlotte's fingers. The things you do for blood are admirable, brother. I admit it," I said, pleased I seemed to be holding my own when it came to cutting Damon down. Every time I did that, I felt a slight increase in respect from Damon. It wasn't a lot, but it was something. And if there was one thing I'd learned from dealing with Damon, it was that Damon only played games by his rules.

"And I'm not obsessed, I'm concerned. And you know

why!" I said. I still felt Damon was hiding something. Or if he wasn't hiding anything, then he certainly wasn't doing anything to let me in. "I know you and I have a history together. An awful, bloody history. But I am raising the white flag. All I want, if we can't be friends, is for us to not be enemies. Not when there's too much at stake for both of us."

"Save the speech." Damon yawned. "I've heard it all. I'm so *bored* with talking! Talk, talk, talk. And it never changes. I have had the same conversations with the same types of people over and over again. I'm bored, brother," he said, looking at me straight in the eye.

"All right then," I said finally. It wasn't an apology by any stretch of the imagination, but what I hoped Damon meant was that he was bored of his vow, that even if he had no interest in resurrecting our bond, at least he no longer felt the urge to carry on a feud. "So let's figure this out. I'm worried about Jack the Ripper because I think he could be an Original. I think he could be Klaus. And he's after us. Or, more likely, he's after you. He must be. Because that note, in blood . . ." I trailed off, trying to somehow get Damon to recognize the importance of it. "It's not just a prank. It looked like the message on the wall at the Sutherlands'. So what does that mean?"

Damon waved his hand in front of his face as if he were swatting a fly. "It means you're vampire-obsessed, brother.

Why would Klaus only kill one woman at a time if he could kill dozens? And why would he toy with the press that way? It all seems very *human*," he said derisively.

"But 'From hell' . . ." I prodded.

Damon rolled his eyes. "For someone who always had his nose in a book, you take things far too literally. I suggest you stop playing detective. Why not have fun? You have a lovely girl, you're in a new city . . . lighten up." Damon looked at me critically. "Or maybe *fill up*. When was the last time you fed?"

"Last night," I said evasively.

"But not on your girl," he remarked, squinting at Violet. I followed his gaze to her white, unmarked neck.

"Of course not." I shook my head. "I don't feed on humans."

"Well, you should. It'll quiet your mind. Think about it. You could forget about this nasty Ripper nonsense and enter London society. You could have fun, more fun than you've ever known."

I sighed, imagining what it would be like: endless parties, endless kisses, endless years of amusement. It was the life Damon had chosen. I felt a flicker of doubt. Could Damon be right? Was the secret to eternal happiness just doing what felt good in the moment?

"Tell you what, brother," Damon said, sensing my hesitation. "Go to Paris. Take yourself away from this nasty business. If it's Klaus, he'll find you wherever you are, and if it's a stupid human, he'll be caught within a few weeks."

"And if it's *you?*" I asked pointedly.

"If it's me, then it was clearly while I was under the influence of copious amounts of alcohol-saturated blood." Damon rolled his eyes. "Come on, brother. Give me some credit. Why would I commit such messy murders in such an undesirable area?"

I nodded. He had a point. And he also had a point that maybe the best thing for me to do for my own peace of mind was simply to go away. But that wasn't possible. I couldn't leave London until I felt Violet was safe. And Violet wouldn't be safe until Jack the Ripper was found. I shook my head.

"Violet has to work at the tavern tonight. I'm going to accompany her, to see if I can find any more information." I paused. "Come with me."

"Come with you? To some rat-infested pub? No thank you."

"You say you're bored. You say it's the same thing every time. Why not do something different? Besides . . ." I took a deep breath. "You owe me."

Callie.

I didn't have to say her name. I saw something flicker in Damon's eye. "Fine. But I'll be drinking champagne, and you're buying."

I grinned. "No champagne, brother. Just ale."

"Good God, do they know nothing about civilization in Whitechapel? Fine. I'll enjoy an ale."

I blinked, sure that I'd heard wrong. But Damon had the same slight smile he'd always had lately, his blue eyes reflecting my face in their inky pupils.

"Does that mean you'll come?" I asked, surprise evident in my voice.

"Sure." Damon shrugged. He turned on his heel, about to rejoin the party, before he glanced back at me.

"Thank you," I said after a beat. "The Ten Bells, in Whitechapel. Meet me at ten. And be careful."

"'Be careful,'" Damon mocked. "Why? In case I meet a vampire on my way? A diversion would be welcome. Like I said, I'm bored *to death*." Damon moved back into the crowd.

I followed him slowly. Damon was doing my bidding. I should have been happy. So why couldn't I ignore the knot in the pit of my stomach?

10

Somehow, I got through the rest of the party. The only thing that saved me from my obsessive thoughts was Violet. She was enchanted by everything, and Damon's friends seemed equally enchanted by her. They thought her accent was bewitching, and Charlotte and her actress friends enjoyed the hero worship that Violet bestowed upon them. Damon, for his part, kept his distance, and spent the majority of the party smoking with Samuel on the sidelines. I sat apart from everyone, reading the letter from the killer over and over again, hoping there was some clue in the words. The Ripper had sent the letter along with what he'd said was a kidney of one of his victims. My stomach turned, but not so much as it did when I read the last line of his letter.

Catch me while you can.

It had been addressed to a newspaper reporter, so the killer had to have known that the letter would appear in the paper. Was it some sort of coded message for me, or Damon? Was it a challenge?

And was I up for it?

That's what I didn't know as I sat in the Ten Bells that night. I'd escorted Violet to her shift, not wanting her to venture across London in the dark on her own. She'd insisted on wearing her new dress so she'd be prepared if we received a last-minute invitation to a party from Damon. But even though she was wearing an apron, the dress was already covered in stains from beer and whiskey. I could tell she was miserable. But at least she was safe.

I shifted uneasily in my chair and glared darkly toward the entrance. Every time the bell would ring announcing a new client I perked up, sure it was Damon, only to see yet another drunk builder or overly perfumed woman stagger in. Of course he wasn't going to come. I'd been foolish to believe him, and more foolish still to have sat waiting for him for the past several hours. When would I stop trying to depend on him?

"Hi, Stefan. Would you like anything?" Violet asked as she trudged toward my table, her shoulders slumped morosely. Her hair was sweaty and pulled back, her lipstick had smeared, and she looked nothing like her glamorous American actress alter ego. Worse still, she knew it.

"A dark ale, please," I said when I caught her eye. I offered a smile, but it didn't make a difference in her mood.

She nodded. "I can't wait to get out of here," she said, her voice dropping to a whisper. "Before, I never knew what I was missing, so it didn't seem so terrible. But now, knowing everyone is drinking and dancing while I'm here . . ." She sighed, her pale pink lower lip trembling.

"All that glitters is not gold," I murmured, pulling a half-remembered Shakespeare phrase from my memory. Something about the language soothed me, and I hoped it would soothe Violet.

"All that glitters is not gold," Violet said, testing out the phrase. She smiled wryly. "That's pretty," she said, half to herself. "I don't mean to complain, it's just . . ."

"I know," I said. "But this won't last forever."

"How do you know? Stefan, this is who I am. I can pretend and dress up, but that's just playacting. This is real," she said sadly. "I'll get your drink," she said as she turned and walked off.

I thought of what she'd said. She was wise for her age. Wasn't I still learning the same lesson?

I leaned back in my chair. About an hour ago, when Violet was busy serving a large group of men playing poker, I'd stolen outside to hunt. Just on the edge of Dutfield Park,

I'd managed to kill a fat pigeon by catching it unawares as it pecked on a filthy crust of bread lodged in the cobblestones. The sour taste stuck to my taste buds. The blood had been cold and thin, and I'd had to resist the urge to gag, but it was the sustenance I needed to make me stop staring longingly at the sleek necks of the ladies circulating the tavern.

Over the din, I heard the bell signaling another customer's entrance. I didn't even bother to look up. Of course it wouldn't be Damon. He didn't care about the killings, and it was clear he didn't care about Klaus or any of the Originals. He was perfectly content getting drunk and feeding off Charlotte. Maybe that was better . . .

"Murder!" A red-faced man staggered in, his bulk practically falling against the bar. He was the same drunk from the other night who had claimed to know me. I felt my stomach clench as the tavern became quiet as a church. "Murder!" he croaked again. "In the square!"

The man collapsed, women shrieked, and before I could stop myself, I was moving at vampire speed out of the bar, knocking over one of the tables as I did so. When I emerged on the street, the scent of iron was everywhere, filling my nostrils and causing my chest to burn. The scent was coming from the east. I took off toward it, already feeling my fangs bulge, pushing away any fear from my brain.

Then I pulled up short at the sight in front of me. There,

just a few paces away, lit by the moon and crumpled on the ground, was a girl in a red dress. Her skirts were askew, her upturned face was pale, and her blue eyes were fixed toward the sky. I recognized her as one of the girls who'd been in the tavern two nights ago. I sank to my knees by her side, relieved when I saw her chest rising and falling.

I licked my fangs and leaned down, eager to taste the warm, rich blood trickling from her neck and matting into her hair. The trail glittered like liquid rubies, and I wanted more than anything to just have a taste, a second to quench my never-ending hunger.

"No," I said out loud, willing my rational brain to take control over my instincts. I leaned back on my heels, the spell between my nature and her blood broken. I knew what I had to do to save her. Without flinching, I brought my wrist to my mouth and ripped my flesh with my fangs. Wincing, I pressed the wound to the girl's pink lips.

"Drink," I said, glancing up to see if there were any signs of commotion. I'd gotten to the girl far faster than anyone would have if they were traveling at normal, human speed, but it wouldn't be long before more bystanders from the tavern found us. And I couldn't have anyone see what I was doing. But without my blood, she'd die.

Far off in the distance, I heard the loud, clanging bells of a police wagon. I needed to leave soon. If the police saw me in this position, they'd assume that *I* was the attacker.

"*Drink*," I said even more forcefully, pushing my wrist up against the girl's open mouth.

The girl coughed before greedily sucking on my wrist.

"Shhh, that's enough," I said, pulling my arm away and hoisting her into a sitting position.

Just then, I saw a shadow hulking behind us. I whirled around, fear icing my veins. Brick buildings surrounded the alley, boxing us in.

"Who goes there?" I asked, my voice echoing off the walls of the alley.

Then, I heard a long, low, all-too-familiar laugh, and Damon strolled around the corner, a lit cigar in his mouth.

"Saving the day again," he said, a bemused grin on his face. He dropped the cigar on the ground, and the ashes glinted in the darkness. Next to me, the girl stirred, moaning and sighing as though she were in the grips of a terrible nightmare.

"He's *here*," I said, my voice falling to a whisper.

"Who, the murderer?" Damon dropped to his knees and glanced at the girl. His fingers brushed against the wound on her neck. "This is amateur work. Just a baby vampire who doesn't know better. If we find him, we'll stake him for the pesky trouble he's causing. But he's not a threat," Damon said, smiling as he wiped a trickle of blood from the side of the girl's mouth.

"More . . ." the girl gasped, clawing the empty air in

front of her. "More!" she yelled in a strangled cry, before collapsing back against the pavement.

"My type of girl." Damon smiled. "Sadly, no more. Stefan's decided you've had enough," he said in a singsong voice. "Stefan always likes to control people," he added cryptically.

I glanced at him in suspicion. Could this have been a trap set up by *Damon*? He'd done it before—half-killed a girl, only to ensnare me into rescuing her. That had been back in New York City, shortly before Klaus and Lucius had beaten Damon at his own game, nearly killing both of us in the process. I was about to remind him of that when a wavering shadow caught my eye.

It was the figure of a man, wearing a top hat, all the way at the far end of the alley. I shot up.

"Did you see that?"

Damon nodded, his eyes widening slightly. "Go. I'll take care of her."

I made a split-second decision to trust my brother. He was all I had.

I lunged toward the shadow, only several meters away from where Damon and I were crouched over the girl.

The shadow bolted as well, stealing around the corner toward the river. I took off after it. My legs were pumping like pistons, and I was running faster and faster, my feet barely hitting the cobblestones. Still, the figure stayed ever so slightly ahead of me, darting this way and that, closer to the rushing Thames.

Faster, I whispered to myself, willing myself to run. Buildings were passing me in the blink of an eye, and I knew I was going as fast I possibly could. Debris blew in my face and caused my eyes to burn, and wind was whistling by my ears. Still, no matter how fast I urged myself to run, I couldn't catch up to the shadow's creator, a tall, thin man who I now knew without a doubt was no human.

We ran, faster and faster, toward the river. I could hear a mob of people far off in the distance, but I didn't look over my shoulder. All my attention was directed at the shadowy man, who was speeding up with every step. The river was now in full sight, the moon casting a dull sheen on the pitch black water. We were one hundred yards away, then fifty . . . would he jump?

"Stop!" I called, my voice ringing like a clarion bell in the darkness. My feet hit the uneven boards of a dock, but the vampire had disappeared. An abandoned pier stood on one side of me, a warehouse on the other, but no sign of the killer. Police bells were clanging from the alleys. I gazed wildly in all directions.

"Show yourself!" I called. My gaze fixed on the warehouse. Could he have ducked in there? I picked my way toward it, stepping on an overturned milk crate to get a view inside one of the windows.

The window was frosted and filthy. I squinted, but even with my heightened senses, I couldn't make out anything within, though I knew the vampire was in there. He had to be. I didn't want to break in and find myself in a death trap. And I knew that if I stayed here, the police would soon find me—and the vampire. A cornered vampire could easily take on the police, and that would lead to more bloodshed. But I couldn't go into the warehouse on my own. There was nothing to do except turn back and get Damon to devise a plan.

I kicked the side of the warehouse in frustration, but then I heard a sound. It was so subtle, I thought it was the waves of the river lapping against the dock until I realized that wasn't it at all.

It was the sound of laughter.

Turning, I trudged back to the tavern.

Unlike an hour earlier, a sober atmosphere had taken over at the Ten Bells when I returned. Candles had been lit, brandy had been poured, and almost every table was occupied by a policeman taking a report from the various revelers who'd been in the tavern when the drunk had come in screaming bloody murder.

"I saw the girl. She was lying in her blood," the man kept saying, his face red. "I *told* you, there was no one else."

Eliza walked up to me, holding a snifter of brandy.

"I was worried about you!" she said. "You ran out, and I thought, that bloke's going to get himself killed, he is. 'Ow's Martha doing?" she asked.

"I don't know," I said. Martha must have been the girl. Had Damon brought her back? I caught a glimpse of Violet, filling brandy glasses as quickly as she could behind the bar. Her face was white with fright.

"Violet!" I called, relieved to see her. "Where is the girl? Is she alive?" I asked brusquely.

"U-u-upstairs," she stuttered, sounding scared and exhausted. "Damon took her up to my old chambers. The d-d-doctor is supposed to be here any minute," she explained.

"Very good," I said. I clasped her hand and she flinched, clearly on edge. "I'm sorry. I want to let you know . . ."

"What?" Violet asked.

"Where's your vervain?" I asked, suddenly in a panic.

"'Vervain'?" she parroted.

"Yes. The charm I gave you."

"It's here!" Violet said, pulling it out of her pocket. "It's a rough crowd here, so I don't like wearing jewelry. But I do like it."

"Good. I was afraid you'd lost it," I said. I leaned down and planted a kiss on her forehead. "Stay brave," I said.

"Okay," Violet said, eyes wide, without any idea of what she was agreeing to.

Hurrying upstairs, I clambered the wooden steps two at a time until I reached a door that led to a tiny room with a slanted roof. Two thin cast-iron beds were on opposite sides of the room, and a single candle was burning in a pewter holder that was precariously placed on an overturned orange crate. Damon was nowhere to be found. In the melee, everyone seemed to have forgotten about Martha. She was lying alone on one of the beds. Although her neck had been bandaged, blood was still seeping out of the wound, forming a sticky red puddle by her ear.

I perched on the edge of the tattered flannel coverlet and smoothed my cracked hand against the girl's forehead. It didn't take a doctor to know that she was still deathly ill. Her breath would catch, then she'd gasp. All I could hear was an ever so faint *thump-da-thump* coming from her chest.

I looked down at my wrist. Already, the wound I'd created less than an hour ago had faded. But although the mark had healed, I still felt depleted, and I knew I had to be very careful with my own reserves of blood. Even so, she needed something more than I'd given her. I brought my other wrist to my mouth and dug my teeth into my flesh, flinching as I felt my mind go woozy.

"Here," I said, cradling the back of the girl's head in my hand. "Drink." I put my wrist up to her lips.

Guided by instinct, the girl tentatively began to suck until I pulled my wrist away. Her head lolled back, and a smile of sleepy satisfaction played on her lips.

Just then a door opened and a man wearing a white coat walked in, carrying a basin of water.

"Are you a friend?" he asked firmly.

"I'm Stefan," I said, putting my hand behind my back and pressing it into the fabric of my coat, hoping he wouldn't notice my wound. "I found her."

"Very well," the man said. "You can stay for a moment, but I'll need some time alone with the patient."

"Yes, of course," I said, relieved he didn't find it odd I was up here. The girl was starting to stir. She'd wake up soon. I hung back as he approached, wanting to make sure she was all right.

The doctor took a towel and dipped it into the basin, then held it against the girl's forehead. As her eyes snapped open, they locked with mine. Then, her features froze and an unholy shriek emerged from her lips.

"Murderer!" she screamed.

The doctor pulled away in shock, almost dropping the basin. His eyes went immediately to the door, as if he was considering yelling for help.

"Shhh, you're safe," I hissed. "I'm your friend. I'm her friend!" I added desperately, turning to the doctor.

"Murderer!" she yelled again, tears springing from her eyes. "Help!"

"She must be in shock," I said to the doctor, hoping there was a medical explanation for her behavior, and not what I feared: that she thought *I* was her attacker.

The doctor nodded, although I couldn't be sure he wasn't just agreeing to appease a suspected criminal.

A starry blackness was forming at the edge of my brain, threatening to overtake me into a faint, but I summoned all my strength. She needed to calm down. Whether she thought I was the murderer because she remembered me kneeling by her side, saving her, or whether she thought I was the murderer because someone had compelled her to think that way, I needed to correct her.

"Listen to me," I said to the girl, forcing my Power into the words. She stopped mid-scream. The room was suddenly so quiet you could hear a pin drop. "I'm your friend. I'm Stefan. I found you. I saved you. You're safe now. There's no murderer here." It took everything I had to keep my gaze on the girl. Thankfully, her weakened state made the compulsion possible. She nodded, then turned to look at the doctor.

"Good girl," I murmured.

"She's all yours," I told the doctor. I had just narrowly escaped that one and I didn't want to push my luck by staying a second longer. The look on his face made me think compelling him wouldn't be necessary. He was starting to relax and get back to his work.

I marched down the stairs and into the tavern, where I caught sight of my brother, laughing as if he'd never been more amused in his life.

11

Entering the main part of the tavern, I headed to the bar to get a drink and collect myself. Had Martha been compelled to believe I'd attacked her? Had *Damon* compelled her? It was possible, and the more I thought about it, the more it made sense. She'd barely even opened her eyes before she blamed me. And she hadn't listened to me at first, she'd simply screamed, as if she'd been primed to do so. There were only two people that could have compelled her to think that way: the vampire I chased to the docks, or Damon, after I'd left her with him.

I ordered a whiskey and turned back to the tables. I could question one suspect right now.

"Hello, brother!" Damon said pleasantly, holding his glass out to me as a form of greeting. "I'm afraid the excitement distracted you from your duties for the evening. I believe you were in charge of the bar tab?" he asked expectantly. "I had a few more whiskeys than I'd intended, but I think they're justified, given the circumstances."

"Why did you do it?" I hissed as I slid into the chair opposite him. I kept thinking of the girl's thin, reedy scream.

"Do what?" Damon asked innocently, taking another sip of his drink.

"You know what I'm talking about," I said darkly.

"No, I don't, actually. I'm sorry if I was unsatisfactory in playing nursemaid to some no-name girl. How was your killer-catching?" he said, arching an eyebrow.

I'm not playing games. And I don't care if you don't want to help, but I know the killer is a vampire, I said under my breath, in a voice low enough that only Damon could hear. If anything, I thought I saw a vague flicker of surprise cross his eyes. *I couldn't catch him.*

So what? Damon asked after a pause. *In all your years roaming you never encountered another one of us, except for the vampire freak house you and Lexi lived in down in New Orleans? You always seem so surprised. We kill, brother. It's nothing novel. Or particularly interesting. The only thing interesting about this is seeing you learn this lesson, over and over again. Hasn't this finally taught you not to meddle? No one appreciates it. Not humans, and not vampires*, Damon said, still smiling.

A chill crept up my spine. Had Damon framed me for the murders? Had *that* been his grand plan? Because he knew that I'd try to help. I couldn't stop myself from getting far too involved in human problems.

I don't seek out problems, I said simply. *And I don't create them.*

Well, maybe you should. They can be fun. Of course, this problem is stupid and careless and blood-drunk, leaving us to clean up his dirty work, Damon mused. "But what's the point?" Damon asked in his normal voice.

"What do you mean?" I asked.

"So you find him. Then what?" he asked, steepling his fingers, then resting his chin against them.

"Then I . . ." I floundered. Would I kill him? Bring him to the police?

Damon looked at me with a bemused expression. "See? You used to think too much. Now you don't think at all. I always thought it would do you good to be more impulsive, but your impulsivity is getting you nowhere. And you know why?" he asked, leaning in close toward me, so much so that I could smell rich, sweet blood on his breath. But was it Charlotte's blood? Or Martha's? Or could it be someone else's entirely?

"Why?" I asked. The scent of the blood was overwhelming.

"Because you're not doing it for yourself. You're doing it

for humanity. For the greater good," Damon said, sarcasm dripping from his voice. "But remember, we're not part of humanity anymore."

"So then why are you constantly compelling yourself into social circles and playing stupid tricks on people? Why are you insistent on being Damon the duke, or Damon the viscount? If we're not part of humanity, why don't you remove yourself from society?" I asked. Despite my words, I wasn't angry at him. Rather, I just wanted to understand what Damon was after.

"Where would I go?" Damon asked, a faraway expression on his face. But all of a sudden, he grinned making his searching look seem to be nothing more than a trick of the light. "And I compel myself into social circles because I can. Because it intrigues me. And my pleasure is all that matters."

"Is that so?" I hissed. I noticed that he didn't follow up that statement with how his other drive in life was to make mine a living hell, but I refrained from mentioning it.

"Yes. Well, brother," Damon said suddenly, draining his whiskey and smacking his lips. "This has been a diverting evening, but if you'll forgive me, I have dinner plans."

"Fine," I said, not wanting to hear what his evening plans entailed. As Damon stood up to leave the tavern, Violet sidled up to us.

"Are you leaving already?" Violet asked, frowning.

"I'm terribly sorry, but as I was saying to Stefan, I have a dinner appointment that I couldn't possibly miss," Damon said, standing and kissing her hand.

"But it's so late." Violet pouted.

"Yes, but I'll see you tomorrow. Won't I, dear?" Damon asked.

"The dock party at Canary Wharf! Of course!" Violet smiled.

The docks? Perhaps the runaway shadow from earlier would be there, if those invited included the undead.

"It'll be a party to die for," Damon said with a knowing smile that caused my skin to crawl. That was the problem: When we were humans, Damon had his dark side, but he was always himself. Now, I had no idea where the real Damon was, or what I should believe.

"We'll be there," Violet said firmly.

"See you later, brother," Damon said as he sauntered out the door without a backward glance.

I stood up too, a wave of dizziness washing over me.

"Let's go, Violet," I said.

She nodded, not bothering to tell Alfred she was leaving. It didn't matter. The tavern felt like an outpost of the police station. In fact, most of the patrons were now police officers, going through their notes and trudging upstairs to check on Martha. Occasionally they'd look over at me and scribble something in their notebooks. I couldn't stay any longer.

Violet hooked her arm in mine and we made our way back toward our hotel. Violet was silent and drawn, caught up in her own thoughts. I knew tonight's events just reminded her of Cora, and I didn't have the words to comfort her, not anymore.

"Are you okay?" Violet asked in a small voice as we stepped onto the dark, plush carpet of the hotel. She was so sweet to be concerned about me at a time like this, I felt my heart almost break.

I forced myself to smile.

"I will be," I said. But she knew I was lying. Death surrounded me, and it was only a matter of time before it caved in—or I broke free. Regardless, there would be blood.

"The trouble with you, Stefan, is that you don't understand death."

I was in the bare bedroom of the carriage house in Mystic Falls. Katherine was clad only in a nightshirt, her figure clearly visible beneath the gauzy fabric. Her dark hair was tied in a loose braid. I ached to touch the silky strands and yet hung back, afraid that once I allowed my hands to roam her body I would lose control. And I didn't want to lose control. Not yet.

"Tell me what death is then," I said. It had been in the days after my fiancée, Rosalyn, had died. Talking with Katherine had allowed me to forget my guilt and step into a world infused with a lemon-ginger scent where nothing—not my father, not Damon, not death—could touch us. It was a world that made me feel safe. Outside the window, I

could see the full moon reflecting on the pond at the edge
of the estate. All of the lights were out in the main house.
There wasn't a cloud in the sky. This was my heaven.

"Where do I begin?" Katherine asked, running her
tongue over her pointed teeth. I automatically brought
my hand up to my neck. It was still tender to the touch,
and a jolt of pleasure mixed with pain occurred whenever
I applied pressure to the place where Katherine had sunk
her fangs.

"Tell me what you know," I said, ever the eager stu-
dent. I kept my eyes on her as she paced back and forth
across the room, as light on her heels as a cat.

"Well, it's in the eye of the beholder. Take your fair
Rosalyn, for example," Katherine said, cocking her head
and staring at me.

"What do you mean?" I'd asked. I wanted to know how
Katherine had evaded death. I didn't know why she was
bringing up Rosalyn. She knew I was supposed to still be
in mourning for the girl who'd never have the opportunity
to be my wife. And in my own fashion, I did mourn for her.

"Well, you remember her, right? What she looked like
and what she smelled like?" Katherine asked in a singsong voice.

"Of course I do," I said, affronted.

"So how is she dead if she lives in your mind?"
Katherine asked, widening her brown eyes at me.

I sighed at her existential meanderings. I stepped toward her, eager to stop talking.

Thankfully, Katherine took my hint. She reached toward me and teasingly grazed her canines across my neck, just enough to leave a scratch.

"That's all I'm saying, Stefan. No matter what happens, in each other, we will live forever," she said. She sank her teeth into my skin as I closed my eyes, the world fading to black as I gave myself to her.

My eyes snapped open. I wasn't entirely surprised I'd dreamt about Katherine. When my life was going well, it was as if all my memories of Katherine existed in an attic of my mind, one that I could go years without visiting. But when things were tough, she was everywhere. The question I still couldn't answer was if I would ever escape her pull, or if she would always be there, lingering in the shadows.

But now wasn't the time to think about that. It was almost time to pick up Violet from the tavern and escort her to the dock party. I'd debated whether or not to let her come. I hoped the party would give me a chance to further explore where the vampire might be hiding, with a chance to fade back into the crowd should he be looking for me. And I didn't want Violet to be where the killer could be. But then I realized that she possessed a fierce amount of determination, and would certainly attend whether or not I wanted her to.

At least I knew she would be safe with me. By making sure that one life wasn't snuffed out by evil, maybe her soul could be a grain of sand, a tiny weight to counterbalance the senseless death and destruction I'd enacted in my past.

At least I could hope.

I massaged my temples. I'd had a constant headache for the past few days, as persistent and buzzing as cicadas on a hot July day. It had only gotten worse the longer I'd been in London. I stood up and crossed over to the glass. My reflection looked pale and drawn, and my eyes were bloodshot. I looked sick, both for a human and a vampire. Reflexively, I touched my fingers to my neck, my mind drifting back to my dream. The faint breeze rustling her white nightdress, the flicker of the lamp against the white-washed walls, the exquisite pain of Katherine's teeth sinking into my flesh . . . everything had seemed so real. But of course, beneath the pads of my fingers was nothing except smooth skin.

Katherine had been dead—*dead* dead, not just mortally dead—for twenty years. Her body had been burned in a church. And yet she was everywhere, as much a part of me as Damon. She'd been right. And back then, I'd been such a fool that I hadn't understood the implications of her words at all.

I walked to the washbasin and splashed cold water on my face, shocked by how much grime and soot disappeared

in the trickle of water. London was a filthy city. But washing the dirt from my face did nothing to scrub the blackness
from my soul.

Noticing the sun sinking fast, casting shadows on the
wall, I quickly finished cleaning up and tied my tie. Hastily,
I made the now-familiar trek across the city. I hated how
on edge I felt, how I viewed every face that passed with
suspicion.

Violet was waiting at the door of the Ten Bells, wearing
the same emerald-green dress she'd worn to the theater
a couple of nights ago. She'd drawn kohl liner around her
eyes, and her mouth was painted a bright red. While the
dress had looked lovely the night at the theater, at the tavern it looked almost garish, and it would be all too easy for
her to be mistaken for one of the ladies of the night. Or
worse, the ideal target for an unholy killer.

"Ready to go?" I asked Violet as I approached, offering
her my arm. She nodded and took it, telling me about her
day at the tavern as we quickly made our way through the
cobblestoned streets toward the dock. On our route several laborers whistled at Violet. I glared at them, cringing
internally. I felt like we were moving targets for anyone in
our path.

As we grew closer, music drifted up from one of the warehouses. It was cheerful, dance hall music and the bustle surrounding the warehouse was at odds with the desolation I'd

seen last night. London reminded me of a kaleidoscope, a child's toy Lexi had picked up once. With one twist, the picture at the other end of the tube changed, and you could never anticipate what you'd see next. I just hoped that the unfolding scenes for Violet and I would be pleasant and not macabre.

"Here we are! Stefan, come on!" Violet said, quickening her stride as she caught sight of a trio of well-dressed men walking toward one of the dimly lit warehouses that lined the dock.

I accelerated my pace until we were even, and then lightly threaded my arm through hers, not wanting to lose sight of her once we entered the party. Several boats were bobbing in the water, and the dock was as crowded as the West End streets after a show let out. The breeze carried the sound of music and laughter toward us.

Violet and I stood outside the bolted metal door and, with a sly glance back at me, Violet brazenly raised her hand as if to knock. But before she could, the door slowly opened.

"If it isn't Miss Burns!" a smooth voice said, and I glanced up. On the other side of the door stood Samuel, wearing a white shirt buttoned to the top and a dark dinner coat hanging off his square shoulders.

"Thank you ever so much." Violet blushed and curtseyed as Samuel offered his arm to her.

"Hello," I politely greeted Samuel. Although as far as I could tell, I'd never done anything to offend him, Samuel always seemed distant toward me. I assumed it was because of my station in life, that he could see from my callused hands and the stubble on my cheeks that I was not used to his world. I suppose I should have simply felt happy he didn't apply that derision to Violet, but still, the snub irritated me. Maybe I did understand a bit why Damon desperately wanted to be accepted by society.

"Stefan," Samuel said, a slight smile crossing his face. "So glad you could make it." I didn't seem to be the only one forcing myself to be polite tonight.

The air was thick with the scent of competing perfumes and cigarette smoke. Candleholders were precariously perched on any flat surface, and it was a miracle that no fires had started. Still, the entire warehouse was dim, making it impossible to tell who was who unless you were standing right in front of them. In the corner, a band was playing a brass-heavy tune I didn't recognize that seemed to thump in rhythm with my head. I'd been wrong in worrying about Violet's dress being inappropriate. The majority of women were wearing dresses with low-cut bodices, the skirts cutting in snugly at their hips. It was a mingling of two distinct London worlds, and it seemed that here was a place where social niceties and decorum didn't matter.

Suddenly, I heard a high-pitched shriek. I whirled around, my fangs bulging, ready to attack.

But all I saw was Violet at the center of the room, hugging a tall, thin girl as if she never wanted to let her go.

"Stefan!" Violet called, waving me over, her eyes shining. "See, I was right. I *knew* she was alive. This is Cora!" she said.

"Cora?" I asked incredulously, taking in the girl in front of me. The crowd had parted somewhat to watch the drama unfold.

Cora nodded, her pale blue eyes seeming hazy and unfocused.

"Yes," she said simply. "I'm Cora." Her voice seemed slow and syrupy. Had she been compelled? I had no idea, no point of reference for how she usually acted. But I felt deeply unsettled. Something wasn't right with this reunion. It was too convenient after so much searching.

"Are you all right? Where have you been?" I asked, trying not to sound like a concerned father. I didn't want to frighten her. After all, we were complete strangers. But I had to know.

Violet seemed oblivious to my questions and was stroking Cora's hair as if she were a favorite pet. "This is Stefan," Violet explained. "My new best friend. I have *so* much to tell you . . ." Violet spontaneously threw her arms around Cora's neck. Cora, like Charlotte, was wearing a silk scarf knotted tightly at the nape of her neck.

"Where were you?" I asked again, my concern reaching desperation. I couldn't make out Damon in the crowd of revelers, but I was sure he was close.

"Where was I?" Cora asked, confusion in her voice. I felt my stomach free-fall.

"Why does it matter?" Violet asked. "The main thing is, Cora's safe, isn't that true?" Violet reached behind her neck and unclasped her pendant. I was about to tell her to keep it on when she hooked it around Cora's neck. The gold of the pendant gleamed in the candlelight.

"This is your don't-go-away present, you hear me?" Violet said, a film of tears covering her eyes. Cora nodded, but she didn't seem to be listening. She was glancing over Violet's shoulder, clearly looking for someone. And while she seemed happy to see Violet, she wasn't overjoyed and didn't seem to fully recognize that she'd been lost.

She kept blinking and tugging the chain around her neck. I watched, entranced. Had she been compelled?

Just then, Damon sauntered up, carrying a bottle of champagne in one hand and champagne flutes in the other. Trailing him were Samuel and a tall man with short blond hair, wearing a top hat and suit.

"I've heard that there's cause for celebration," Damon said as he suavely popped the cork from the bottle. It exploded with a festive fizzing sound, and he began pouring glasses.

"This is my sister!" Violet explained, not tearing her gaze off of Cora.

"How nice," Damon said, leering. "Family reunions are lovely. And I knew I liked something about you," Damon said, draping his arm around Violet's shoulder. "Cora joined our little group just recently as well, a friend of Samuel's brother. Now it seems we're just keeping it all in the family!"

"This is *Cora*," I said angrily. "Remember?"

Damon shrugged. "Like I said, not in the newspaper, not in my mind. My memory just gets worse and worse with age!" he exclaimed.

"Shut up," I growled.

"Is that any way to talk to a brother?" Damon responded, keeping a smile on his face.

"Here here!" Samuel said, raising his glass in a toast, unaware that anything was amiss. "To families. Including my own brother, Henry," he said, gesturing to the pale, blond man standing next to him. At first glance, he seemed to be about eighteen or nineteen.

"Pleased to meet you," I said, barely managing a polite tone. But Henry's face cracked into a wide smile, and he pumped my hand enthusiastically.

"Pleased to meet you, too," he said in an aristocratic

British accent that sounded just like his brother's. But his warm and almost naïve expression was nothing like Samuel's—and immediately I noticed him casting his gaze on Violet.

"Hello," he said warmly.

Violet turned to him, her upturned face full of interest. I knew what I was witnessing was the lightning-quick passage of emotions that humans took for granted—the moments at which a stranger became something more, became someone a human could imagine growing old with. In the shadowy darkness, there was no way Henry could tell Violet was a waitress. Violet was speaking in her well-modulated actress voice, and her new dress betrayed none of the stains of the Ten Bells. *This is a remarkable age.* Just like George had told me, maybe Violet truly could transcend her class and find happiness. She deserved it.

Even though Cora had been found and seemed none the worse for the wear, I knew I couldn't leave until I cracked the mystery. Why was Damon being so cagey? There was no way he wasn't somehow involved with the murders. The question was, what had he done? And who had he done it with?

I looked at Henry and Violet again. They were engaged in conversation, their heads bowed as if they'd known each other for years. At least Violet was preoccupied and with someone safe, which gave me the chance I needed to search the party for the mysterious vampire who'd eluded me last night.

Moving through the crowded party proved fruitless. Girls so drunk they could hardly stand up were pawing at me, and the noise of the band overloaded my senses. I stepped outside the warehouse, thinking I would try to find the door he ran through last night. Perhaps he'd left something behind.

The fresh air helped clear my head. I started to walk around the warehouse, looking for a familiar window or door. And then, as the wind picked up, I smelled it.

It was the scent of blood—warm, coursing, and close.

I gnashed my teeth together. The scent made me simultaneously eager to feed and nervous. The killer must be one of the revelers inside the party. But who was he? Or—and this was the thought that filled me with terror— had he already made his move, and the fragrance in the air was a fresh kill?

That possibility was what spurred me to race back inside the warehouse, tearing through the crowd, desperate to find the source of the scent. I didn't have any time to waste. It was as if I'd lived through the same scenario far too many times, always coming to the scene half a second, half a minute, or half a day late. But this time would be different, I thought wildly as I pushed past a dancing couple, the man whirling a woman faster and faster on his arm. I was no longer a "baby vampire," a term Lexi derisively used to use to describe me. I had wisdom, age, and blood behind me. This time, I would stop evil before it started.

The warehouse was deceptively large, and I was shocked that the space kept going and going, each inch of concrete floor filled with people laughing, smoking, and drinking as if they didn't have a care in the world.

"Pardon me!" I yelled in frustration, elbowing my way through couples and treading on people's shoes, only following the ever more pungent scent of iron—until I ran into a solid mass.

I looked up. It was Samuel. Instantly, I stood to my full height and gave him a tight smile. I knew that careening through the warehouse must have made me seem drunk or mad.

"Pardon *you*!" Samuel said jovially, tipping back his whiskey. "You seem to be in a hurry," he added, a flicker of amusement on his face.

"I'm looking for a friend," I muttered, my eyes darting from one side to the other. I realized I hadn't seen Violet while I was running around. Now not only was I searching for a killer, but for an innocent girl as well. I had to make sure she was safe.

"Consider him here!" he said jovially, blocking my path.

"Not you," I said, realizing only after the words left my mouth how rude they seemed. "I mean, I'm looking for Violet."

"Violet!" His eyes lit up in recognition. "Of course. I thought I saw her over by the bar . . . would you like to go with me?"

I didn't bother to be polite as I took off toward the bar, desperately scanning the crowd. It thinned out as I ran, and finally, I could stand without being bumped or jostled. I allowed my eyes to readjust to the dim light. The far side of the warehouse had two open doors that led to the docks, and, beyond that, the water. The doors had been propped open with several wooden milk crates, presumably to allow fresh air in. Still, while the rest of the warehouse was crammed, this part was unlit and deserted. I could smell cobwebs and mold.

And blood.

Outside, the clouds shifted, and a shaft of moonlight reflected through the filthy windows at one end of the warehouse. My eyes fell upon a crumpled heap in the corner. At first, I hoped it was nothing more than a discarded pile of fabric, pushed aside for the party. But it wasn't. The material was bright green.

I blanched, already knowing what I'd see before I turned the figure over.

But when I did, I still couldn't hold in my strangled cry.

It was Violet, her throat slit, her inquisitive blue eyes gazing, unblinking, at the throng of people dancing only yards away from her cold, white figure.

13

I had to get Violet out of there, before the killer came back to finish her off with his customary mutilation. I hastily lifted her up and heaved her over my shoulder. Her body grew colder every minute and the touch of her skin against mine sent a shiver down my spine. She was dead. And the killer was nowhere to be found.

I glanced around wildly. The band had shifted into a waltz, and the front of the warehouse was crowded with couples dancing in the darkness. It looked gaudy, like an act from the two-bit carnival I'd worked at in New Orleans. The murderer was somewhere in that throng, bowing and weaving through couples.

My fangs throbbed, and my legs ached with the urge to run or fight. But I could do neither. I stood, frozen in place.

Droplets of blood scattered across the bodice of her dress, and the kohl she'd used to line her eyes had run, making her face look like it was painted with tears.

I didn't feel sorrow. What I felt was deeper, more primal. I felt anger at whoever did this, as well as despair. This would always keep happening, and more victims like Violet would perish. It wouldn't matter if I journeyed back to America or went to India or just traveled nomadically throughout every land. How many deaths could I witness, all the while knowing death would never come to me?

I glanced back down at Violet's limp body and forced myself to stop thinking those thoughts. Instead, I thought of Violet's short life. Her wide grin when she'd put on one of her fine dresses, the way her happy face shone with tears at the end of the musical review, the way she truly believed that there was good in the world. I'd miss her. Violet had been spritely and passionate and *alive*. She'd also been stupid and trusting and so vulnerable. And she'd given up her vervain to her sister. Of course, she hadn't known it to be anything but a good luck charm, but still—if she'd had the vervain, she'd be alive now.

"'May flights of angels sing thee to thy rest,'" I said, quoting Shakespeare for lack of a prayer as I laid my hand against her cold brow and smoothed her loose curls off her forehead. The phrase echoed in my head, the words far more familiar to me than any of the sermons I'd sat through or psalms I'd heard when I was a human. I leaned down and grazed my lips against Violet's cheek.

Suddenly, she reared up, her body trembling all over, her eyes wide, her mouth frothing, as she lunged toward my hand.

Hastily, I fell backward, scrambling to my feet and retreating to the shadows.

"Stefan?" Violet called in a high and reedy voice that sounded nothing like her Irish brogue. Her hand frantically clawed at her throat, and her eyes widened in fright when she pulled her hand back and saw it covered with blood. "Stefan?" she called again, her eyes gazing wildly in all directions.

I watched in shock. I'd seen death countless times at this point, and I knew that Violet had been dead. Yet now she wasn't. This meant only one thing: She had been given vampire blood and then killed. She was in transition.

"Stefan?" she asked, grasping the air in front of her and gnashing her teeth against each other. Her breath was loud and raspy. She kept licking her lips, as though she were dying of thirst. "Help me!" she called in a strangled voice.

Far off in the warehouse, I could make out the faintest sound of the band striking up another song. Everyone inside the party was blissfully unaware of the gruesome scene occurring in front of my eyes. I clenched my jaw. I wanted more than anything to be strong for Violet, but I was still in shock.

I knew she wanted to feed. I remembered the agonizing hunger I'd felt when I'd woken up in transition. She was breathing in loud, staccato gasps as she rose to her knees, then her feet. I moved forward to help her.

"Shhh," I said, wrapping my arms around her body. "Shhh," I repeated, running my hands through her tangled hair, wet with sweat and blood. "You're safe," I lied. Of course she wasn't.

A few yards away, on a neighboring dock, I saw a small skiff, most likely used to transport cargo from one side of London to the other, bobbing in the gentle waves of the Thames. I had the wild thought to take it, to head as far as we could down the river, to just get away.

"What's happening to me?" Violet gasped each word, clutching her throat.

"You'll be okay, Violet. But please, tell me, who did this to you?" I asked.

"I don't know," she said, her face crumpling. Blood was running from her neck, drying into a pattern on the side of her dress that would have been almost pretty if one hadn't known how it was formed. Her face was white and chalky, and she kept licking her lips. "I was going to the bar. And then he pulled me to him for a dance, and . . . that's all I can remember," Violet said, wringing her hands together and gazing imploringly at me.

"Who's 'he'?" I asked urgently.

"Damon," she said, hardly able to stifle her cries. A scene flitted into my mind: Violet, so excited to have Damon pay attention to her. Violet, allowing Damon to escort her to the bar and order her a drink. Violet, nervous and coquettish, waiting to hear what Damon had to say. And then Damon licking his lips, lunging, and drinking, leaving Violet behind for me to find.

You always help a damsel in distress. Damon's mocking phrase rang in my ears. He'd left her for me to find, just as if we were children playing hide-and-seek.

"I'm so thirsty," Violet said, leaning over the edge of the dock and cupping her hands to capture some of the dirty water flowing in the Thames. I watched as she put her hands to her mouth, and saw an expression of disgust cross her face. She knew something was terribly wrong. "Stefan . . . I don't feel well. I think I need a doctor," she said, cradling her head in her hands and rocking silently back and forth.

"Come with me," I said, pulling Violet into a hug. I could feel shivers wracking her body, and saw tears were falling from her large eyes. I knew she was confused and disoriented, and this filthy dock was no place to explain to her what was happening.

I hoisted her up and walked us to the skiff that was resting in the water. I gently placed her on its floor. She blinked a few times and let out a shuddery sigh.

"Am I dead?" she asked, her hand reaching out toward mine. I closed my fingers over hers. I tried to remember back to my own death. I'd felt hazy and confused as well, coupled with the grief and guilt of losing Katherine. Then, when I'd made the full transition, I'd felt fast, sharp. Inhuman.

"Yes," I said. "You're dead."

Violet flopped back down and closed her eyes.

"It hurts so much," she whimpered as she slumped against the side of the boat in exhaustion. Her body couldn't take the transition.

I felt anger slice through my stomach. Damon needed to pay for this.

I took a piece of muslin, most likely used to repair sails, from the side of the boat and pulled it over her body like a blanket. She was sleeping now, and I knew she didn't have the strength to run off. She sighed and burrowed into the cloth while I jumped off the skiff and tore back into the party.

As soon as I walked back into the smoky warehouse, I could hear my brother's voice above the din, laughing and making fun of the ridiculous expedition Lord Ainsley had planned in India. Not caring who saw me, I used my vampire speed to reach him. He was laughing with Samuel and Henry. Cora clung to his every word.

"You ought to go to India, too, Damon. You're always complaining you've had enough of London society," Henry said, raising his champagne toward Damon. "Maybe an adventure would do you good."

"Yes, you could try your luck at snake charming," Samuel suggested. "You already have proven your talent for charming women."

At this, Damon laughed appreciatively. Fury rose up inside me. How *dare* he laugh and joke only minutes after he'd attacked Violet and set her on the path we'd both regretted taking.

"You," I growled, dragging my brother out by the arm and toward the alley that led down to the docks, empty except for a far-off vagrant sleeping with a bottle of whiskey clutched against his chest.

"Ah, a moonlit conversation by the waterfront. How picturesque. What's the special occasion?" Damon asked, arching a dark eyebrow.

I recoiled. I hated everything about him. I hated his affected Virginia drawl that he put on in my presence as if to make fun of our polite upbringing, the way he twisted words even if he was the only one who'd get the joke, and the way he made a mockery out of everything, including human life.

"You are dead to me," I growled, grabbing him with all my might and throwing him toward the opposite wall, satisfied to hear his skull cracking against the concrete. He slumped, ragdoll-like, before standing up, his eyes flashing in the darkness. He took a quick step toward me, then stopped and laughed softly.

"Someone's found his strength again," Damon said, still rubbing his temple. The wound had closed almost instantaneously, leaving nothing but smooth, pale flesh. "Why so upset? Didn't find the murderer you were looking for?" Damon mocked in a low voice.

"No more games. *You're* the killer!" I spat, rage boiling in my veins. I wanted to hurt him. But the trouble was, nothing would.

"I am, am I?" Damon asked nonchalantly. "Tell me, how did you reach that conclusion, Detective Salvatore?"

So this was how he'd decided to torment me now. No more blows or fights or battles, just psychological torture. Well, he'd succeeded.

"You framed me for the attack the other day. And you killed Violet," I said, my voice clear as a crack of thunder.

A million expressions—hate, anger, annoyance— flashed across Damon's face before he lunged toward me, pinning me against the cold concrete wall, his face only inches from mine. I squirmed to get away, but he only held me harder.

"I've tried to be patient with you, brother," Damon said, hate dripping from his voice. "I thought that maybe a few decades had done us both good. But you're the same as you've always been. Always the one to come into a situation and think he knows how to fix it. Always the foolish knight in shining armor. Always the one who takes responsibility for the whole world on his shoulders. But . . ." Damon's voice dropped to a whisper, so only I could hear. "You are not innocent. You started all of this. And death doesn't begin and end with me. Get used to it, brother. People die, and you can't change it." He let go of my neck, but not before spitting in my face. "Be warned, next time I show up in your life, it won't be all parties and picnics. You can trust me on that." Damon turned on his heel and headed back to the party.

I watched him, fists clenched, still fully aware of the indents on my neck where Damon had pinned me. He was much stronger than I was, and I knew he didn't want me to forget it. My mind lingered on Damon's glee that Violet was dead. Of course, he would never change. He would forever enjoy seeing me in pain. He thought I had wronged him and would continue to destroy anyone I cared about. He would keep killing, and for what? To settle a score against me that could never, ever be settled. Because while I may have turned him into a vampire, he was the one who turned himself into a monster.

But now Violet was transitioning and the only thing I could do to make up for my mistakes was to try to help her through it. I hurried as fast as I could back to the skiff, where I saw slight movement from underneath the muslin cloth.

"Violet!" I said, sinking to my knees next to her.

Her eyes fluttered open, the pupils enormous and cloudy. I pulled her tightly against my body, wishing there was something I could do for her. But the only thing I could do was give her the opportunity to leave this world as she came into it—as a human, without blood on her hands.

"Stefan," she croaked, struggling to sit up.

"We need to go," I said, dragging her to her feet. Damon would be looking for her now to ensure her transformation was complete. I knew I should double back in and find Cora, but I couldn't risk it. I had to hope the vervain was helping Cora when I could not.

I couldn't give Violet much, but I could at least give her a choice—and let her know exactly what would happen with either path she chose. It was an impossible, monstrous choice, but it was hers, and might be the last one she'd ever make. She deserved to do it in peace. I needed to bring Violet somewhere she could be safe.

"Come on," I said, helping her up and holding her close. I began to run, clumsily at first, until I gathered the speed I was accustomed to when I was fully in tune with my Power. Once or twice, I thought I caught a glimpse of a curtain rustling, or a shadow too tall to be my own. I even thought I heard a racing footstep behind me. It only galvanized me to go faster, barely stopping before we reached the street in front of our hotel. I paused. Damon knew where we were staying. It wasn't safe there. I looked down at Violet, who was still disoriented and growing weak.

"The party?" Violet asked, sitting up and holding her hand to her head. "The champagne . . . did I get drunk?" she asked.

I wanted to say yes. I wished I could spare her the pain of the upcoming hours. But she deserved more than that. I hadn't lied to her when I'd found her and I wouldn't lie to her now. I would make sure she knew the choice she faced. It was the least I could do. I thought back to the way her face had shone when she saw the Gaiety Theatre, and an idea formed in my mind.

"Let's go to the theater," I said.

"The theater?" Violet blinked, as though she didn't understand my invitation. I didn't blame her. Her situation was dire, even she knew that, and yet it sounded like I was asking her to a church social.

I nodded and helped Violet to her feet. Together, we hobbled along the deserted cobblestoned sidewalks. It was nearly morning.

The lights in front of the Gaiety were off, but the stage door with its rusted hinges didn't take too much strength to force open. Once we were in the dark theater, I sighed. Finally, I felt we were safe from Damon.

"Is this another party? Because I don't think I'm up for it." My heart twisted at the innocent disappointment in Violet's voice.

I motioned for Violet to sit next to me on one of the crushed red velvet chairs facing the stage.

"I brought you here because I knew how much you loved it. And what I have to tell you won't be easy to process," I explained, blinking in the darkness. It was easier to have this conversation when we weren't facing each other.

"Damon . . ." Violet said, then shuddered. "He was so nice. He introduced me to all of his friends. And then . . ."

"He attacked you," I said dully.

She grimaced, but didn't refute what I'd said.

"I remember drinking champagne. And I was laughing, and then . . . I don't know. It's as if my mind just goes blank," she said, helplessly shaking her head.

I rolled my lapis-lazuli ring around my finger. Back when I had transitioned, Katherine's maid, Emily, had explained what was happening to me. She'd been the one to give me the ring. Katherine had asked her to give one to me and one to Damon. Emily'd been cool, and calm, and had kept her distance while I suffered. I couldn't do that.

"Stefan? What's happening to me?" Violet asked, her voice cracking.

I laced Violet's ice-cold fingers through mine. "You're in transition. You were killed by a vampire," I said. "Damon."

"Vampires?" Violet said, her voice tripping over the word. "That's just from storybooks. What are you talking about?"

"No they're real. I'm a vampire. And so is Damon. He's my brother. My *true* brother," I said, staring straight ahead. I hated what I was saying, but knew it would be far worse to keep the truth a secret. "We look human. Once, we were human. We grew up together, laughed together, and were a family. But not anymore. We survive only because we drink the blood of others. I choose animals. But my brother doesn't."

"Does that mean I'm a vampire now, too, then?" she asked, her voice shaking.

I shook my head. "No," I said firmly. "Damon killed your human body, but gave you some of his blood first. To complete the transition and to fully become a vampire, you have to drink human blood. If you don't, your body will die," I said. The wallpapered room felt like it was closing in on me.

"But, Stefan, I don't understand. If there's a way to live then why . . ." She trailed off, her voice sounding so innocent and lost that I felt my stomach clench.

"Because it's not that simple. Being a vampire is not

like being alive. You're consumed by your desire for blood, your desire to kill. You become a completely different person . . ." I trailed off as Violet pressed her hand to my chest, gently at first, and then more and more insistently. I resisted the urge to pull away. It was an intimate gesture, one you'd imagine between lovers.

"I don't . . . I can't . . ." she said, horror dawning on her face as she continued to graze my chest with her hands. "There's no heartbeat," she exclaimed, now understanding what I'd been trying to tell her.

"No," I said patiently.

"What if I want to . . . turn?" she asked. "What if I want to become like you?"

"I would help you. That's your choice to make. But it's something to think about seriously before you do. It's not a real life. It's not a blessing to live forever. You witness so many people dying, and you're always a creature of darkness. You have to live in the shadows, only emerging at night. And you shouldn't have to live like that," I said, squeezing her hand. "You belong in the light."

Violet's sobs overtook her, and I knew she grasped the reality she faced.

"I was just starting to live . . ." she said wistfully and rubbed her neck gently, as if she were remembering a long-ago caress from a lover. Her hand dropped back to her chest. Then she looked at me, tears in her eyes.

"When?" she asked.

"Soon," I admitted. My eyes darted to the half-open stage door. I could see that the sky was getting lighter. We couldn't stay here. Violet needed to be somewhere safe, and there was nowhere in London that was safe from Damon.

Violet sniffled, and I saw two large tears roll down her cheeks. "I want to go home," she said in a small voice. "I want to be with my mom and sisters. I don't belong here. If I have to die . . . and I want to die, I don't want to become a monster . . . then I want to die as myself. As Violet Burns. I want to be home. I want Cora."

I glanced at her as she stared bravely ahead. I wanted to charter a ship, or to swim across the dark Irish Sea myself to give her what she wanted. But I couldn't. And she knew that.

"I'm just rabbiting on. I just want to see my sister one last time."

"I know you do," I said. "But if we find her, then I think Damon will find you. But Cora's all right. She's protected. The charm you gave her is filled with vervain. It's an herb that protects people from vampires. I didn't tell you because I didn't want to scare you, but . . ."

Violet clawed at the hollow of her neck. "It was my fault," she realized.

"No. You saved your sister. Whether or not you knew what the charm was, you knew it was good luck, and you gave it to her. That's love," I said, smiling at Violet. I wondered if I'd been in a similar situation, if I'd have done the same thing for Damon.

"Well, I hope she thinks of me every time she wears it," Violet said. "And maybe I can write her a letter. And you can deliver it. Because she needs someone to look out for her," Violet said, piecing each sentence together slowly.

"Of course. I'll look after Cora, and I promise you, she will be safe. And I know where I can take you," I decided, picking up her hand. I hoped the Abbotts' farm would remind her of the rolling Irish hills she'd told me about. It was a small comfort, no replacement for the real thing, but it was the best I could do.

Violet nodded meekly. I looked down at her in agony, a tear threatening to escape my eye. I let it fall, watching it splash on Violet's hair, wishing there was something I could do. All I'd wanted this evening was for Violet to be safe. And here she was still in my arms—but full of vampire blood. I had failed her.

14

There have been times in my life that I felt something, or someone, was watching out for me. Because how else could both Violet and I have made it to Paddington Station without being stopped by the police or a concerned passerby? It helped that we took a few garments from a traveler's luggage as they waited for their train, and were no longer wearing bloodstained clothes. But still, I had to support Violet against my side, and even a casual observer could see she was close to death. And yet, no one had noticed us.

I didn't think of it as providence. Maybe I would have, at one point. But now I only felt it was evidence of my innate evil. I frightened people. Tonight, the only ones who might block our path would be monsters.

Once we got to the train station, I used the last few

coins in my pocket to pay for our tickets to Ivinghoe. We caught the first train out of the city, and I should have felt relief. But I didn't. Because I had no idea when Violet was going to die. All I hoped was that I could get her safely to my cabin.

"Stefan?" Violet asked as her fingers, as light as the brush of a hummingbird's wing, glided across my arm.

"Yes?" I replied, pulling my gaze away from the window. Instead of looking like she was at death's door, Violet had a flush in her cheeks and her eyes were bright. We'd been on the train for nearly an hour and were now on the outskirts of London's sprawl. Even a touch of country air was doing wonders for Violet. But it wouldn't save her.

"I feel better," Violet whispered hopefully, obviously thinking the same thing that I had. "Do you think I might live?"

"No," I said sadly. I didn't want to be callous, but it would be even crueler to fill her with false hope. No matter how she felt or how she looked, Violet's fate was sealed.

"Oh," she said quietly, pressing her lips together and staring out at the greenery passing by the window. The compartment we were seated in was identical to the one I had sat in when I came to London. A silver tea-service tray lay between us, with china plates piled high with scones and sandwiches. It was still very early, and the train was almost deserted. Violet had alternated between dozing and taking dainty bites of one of the scones. I'd spent the majority of the journey staring out the window. The scenery was lush and green, and totally at odds with the darkness of my mood.

"Once the transition starts, there's no cure," I repeated patiently.

"Except if I drink human blood," Violet corrected.

"That's not a cure," I said grimly.

"I know," Violet said quietly before staring far off into the distance.

"If I could go back and do it all over again, I would have chosen death," I said. I put my hand on top of hers to comfort her.

"There's so much I haven't seen and haven't done," Violet said sadly. "I was never onstage, I never had children . . . I've never even been in love."

I continued to stroke her small hand. There was nothing I could say.

Violet whimpered and allowed her head to rest against my shoulder. "I'm so cold," she whispered.

"I know. I know," I said. I stroked her hair, wishing I could make her death easier. *It would be*, I told myself. Once we were back at the Manor and away from danger. I wanted her to find solace in the quiet of my cabin and peacefully slip away. She'd had a hard life. Maybe the afterlife would be better for her.

Violet's breathing steadied, and she fell asleep. I glanced out the window. The sky seemed clearer the farther we got from London. I heard a faint noise, but it wasn't coming from my mind. It was coming from outside.

"Yes?" I called sharply, assuming it was a porter arriving with more scones or another selection of papers.

But no one answered. The scratching noise was persistent, louder than just a stowaway rat.

I heard another noise, as if the train had hit a large animal. But the train kept rolling. I glanced out the window and a long, low growl I didn't quite recognize as my own escaped my lips.

There, peering upside down through the window, was Samuel's brother, Henry. His face was pressed to the glass, and his golden-blond hair was blowing in the wind.

We locked eyes, and for one wild moment I thought he'd come to see Violet, an eager beau's overtures gone too far. But then I noticed his elongated canines, his bloodshot eyes, and I slowly understood. *Henry* was a vampire. And Henry wasn't eagerly looking for Violet. He was hunting— for us.

I slammed the blue damask curtains of the window shut and looked around madly for any escape. But of course there was none. I felt my heart harden. This was Damon's doing. It had to be. Because why else would Henry be here? Even as children, he'd goad the Giffin boys into throwing rocks at a passing train or letting the chickens loose during a barbeque. That way, he wouldn't risk punishment. Now, he was doing the same thing, except with a cadre of vampires.

I had to protect Violet. I couldn't let Henry grab Violet and force her to feed. I couldn't have her turn into a vampire against her wishes. I hastily stole to the caboose and climbed the rickety ladder to the top of the iron train. The wind pelted dirt and pebbles into my face, and the soot and fumes whirling around my head made it almost impossible to see anything.

"Henry!" I called, steadying myself on the steam pipe poking from the top of the train. I crouched low, ready for a fight.

Nothing. The train continued to chug forward. A sliver of doubt crept through my brain. Had it been some sort of vision? A paranoid hallucination?

A cry of outrage sounded behind me.

Before I could turn, I felt a weight on my back, followed by cold hands sliding around my neck. I gasped and tried to writhe free from the grip. I was locked in a chokehold, Henry's arm tight around my windpipe. I groaned, trying to fight him off while keeping my balance.

"Are you ready to die?" Henry whispered in my ear. His impeccable accent was perfectly modulated, and his breath was hot against my neck. Once again, he applied pressure to my throat.

Die. The word echoed in my head. I'd forgotten what it was like to be hunted. But now, I was captured. And if I didn't do something, I would die. And Violet would be worse than dead. I had to do something. I had to . . .

Stay still. A voice—Lexi's? My own?—screamed instruction in my head, even though it was counterintuitive to my being's every instinct. My arm twitched beneath Henry's grasp. *Stay still!* the voice insisted.

"Frightened? And you thought I was just little Henry. One of Damon's foppish friends, of no importance and no interest to a big, strong American vampire like yourself. Aren't I right, chum?" Henry asked sarcastically, pulling me closer. He was clearly going to try to break my neck, and from there, he'd be able to stake me or burn me, or do whatever he wanted. Or he could simply throw me off the train, where I'd be finished off soon enough. A dozen scenarios, each worse than the last, whirled through my mind.

"What? You're not going to speak to me?" Henry asked, goading me. I stared at the ground whooshing below me, pulling every ounce of strength from the corners of my being. I thought of Callie, the death I hadn't avenged. I thought of Violet, about to be next.

"This ends now!" I yelled, spinning around, fists ready. I was larger than him, but I knew from the pressure of his arm against my throat that he was stronger than me. I'd have to be faster and smarter.

"Is this the way you want to do this?" Henry half-growled, lunging toward me. I sidestepped him, and my foot began to slip off the train. I reached out, clinging to the steam pipe, as Henry swung his fist. Flesh connected to my temple and for a moment, all I saw were stars.

Henry's low, smooth laugh yanked me out of my fog of pain.

I pretended to totter as though in danger of losing my grip. I wanted to catch Henry unaware. And then I reached back and swung.

Blood gushed from Henry's lip and I stepped back, surveying my work in satisfaction.

"Not as easy as you thought it'd be, is it?" I asked in disgust. Damon had probably told his posse I always avoided conflict, even to my own peril. Well, not anymore. I was done with Damon's games.

Henry retreated a few meters, rubbing his wound and attempting to regain his balance. The wound was fast disappearing, and I knew I needed to act quickly.

I bent my knees, hoping my instincts from decades of jumping with horses would help me. It was all about looking where you were going, and never, ever looking away. I glanced at a small metal dent in the center of the car a few meters away, and jumped.

My body careened through space as I heard Henry growl below me. I didn't look, concentrating on that tiny imperfection on the train's exterior until my feet hit the metal with a *thud*. Then I whirled around and lunged, aiming toward his face, giving him a punch with as much strength as I could muster. My fist connected with his flesh. He stood, his body weaving on one leg, suspended in midair like a dancer awaiting his next cue, before he tumbled off the train. His body landed in a heap on the ground, growing smaller in my view as the train sped on.

"See you in hell," I murmured. To anyone else, it would be a curse. But for me, it was a promise.

I climbed down the rickety ladder and stepped onto the caboose car, hoping against hope that no conductor or policeman would be waiting for me. I was weak and shaky, covered with blood and soot.

I picked my way back to the cabin, relieved that no one stopped me on my way. Violet was still sleeping, her breathing shallow and occasionally interrupted by a gasp, although whether or not that was from pain or a dream, only she knew.

I couldn't sit. Instead, I paced like a wild animal, desperate to do something. So Damon had enlisted Henry to do his dirty work. The question was, were there others? I had the strength to fight off one, but could I fight off several? And would we be able to hide from them for long enough, at least to allow Violet to die in peace?

The train whistle blew, and Violet stirred in my lap. We'd arrived at the tiny Ivinghoe station.

"Wake up," I said, gently rousing her. My temple throbbed, and the wound was slow to heal, a true sign that I was quickly losing strength.

"Stefan," she said sleepily before opening her eyes. "What happened?" She gasped as she took in my appearance.

"We're being followed," I said tersely, glancing past Violet toward my reflection in the window. I looked awful. I looked like I'd been caught in a war. Which, I suppose was more or less what I'd found myself in. "By Henry," I clarified grimly.

"Henry!" Violet gasped again, her face turning pale. "What do you mean?

"He's a vampire, too. Damon has a lot of very powerful friends. But I got rid of him," I explained. I knew it sounded like I'd killed him, and I fervently wished that had been the case. But I had a feeling I'd simply wounded him, and if so, I knew he'd be quick to return. The train whistle blew as we rolled into the train station. "Come with me," I said brusquely.

Violet struggled to her feet and followed me down the narrow aisle of the train car.

"Sir?" a conductor called from behind us. I whirled around, noticing the split second that it took him to see the blood on my hands, the grime and soot all over my clothes.

One more time, I said to myself, locking eyes with him. Just because compelling had become routine over the past few days did not mean it took any less effort. I forced myself to stand still. "You never saw us," I said as the train came to a stop, its brakes squealing.

Violet held my hand tightly and stepped behind me, as though she were a frightened animal being protected by a larger, stronger member of the pack.

I continued to look in the conductor's watery, sleepy eyes. "We're leaving now. And when you pass through the carriage, you won't remember us," I said, walking down the three steps toward the platform. The conductor trailed behind us, leaning over the steps as if unsure whether or not to hop off the train and ask us more questions. I continued to stare.

"I never saw . . ." I heard the conductor agree, before the whistle blew and the train whirred away, heading deeper into the country.

"What happened?" Violet asked, hands on her hips as dust from the departing train whipped around us. She still seemed woozy and was staggering as though drunk.

"It's a power vampires have. I can make people do my bidding. I don't like to do it, but it can come in handy." I hoped I wouldn't have to do any compelling on our three-mile journey back to the manor. Who knew if Mrs. Todd at the post office or Mr. Evans at the general store were peeking out from behind their curtains, wondering what Stefan the groundskeeper was possibly doing with a crying, pale, sick girl. "But we're here, in Ivinghoe. You're safe."

Violet shook her head. "I'm *not* safe," she said, her voice low and faint. "I'm dying." I saw her flinch and realized that the sun must be agonizing to her. Red splotches were dotting her arms and legs, and her face was slicked with sweat. I glanced helplessly at my lapis-lazuli ring, wishing there was something I could do. But I needed to be wearing the ring at all times.

"Let's go," I said, hooking my arm in hers and crossing to the shady side of the street. It wasn't much relief, but it was something. Then, together, we trudged up the winding path to Abbott Manor.

15

By the time we reached the path that led to the Abbott's back garden, my mind had cleared. The woods were beautiful, dark, wild, and mysterious. One of the local legends was that long ago, fairies had settled the land and made it their home, hiding in the ample oak tree trunks and looking out for the forest life. Of course, I didn't believe the tale. I'd been through the woods and captured and killed enough animals to know there were no benevolent creatures protecting the forest. Or if there were, then they had better things to do than save an errant squirrel or rabbit that was caught in the clenches of a vampire's fangs. Still, the story comforted me, if only because it proved that humans could still believe in good, even when so much evil lived in their midst.

We walked toward the clearing, where the sprawling three-story brick manor house rose up on the crest of a hill.

"Here we are," I said, gesturing to the vast expanse, as if I were a king showing off my land to my subject.

"It's nice," Violet said, a small smile creeping onto her pale lips. "Green. It reminds me of home."

I heard the dog bark and I startled. I knew that most likely Luke or Oliver would be nearby, and I didn't want them to see Violet. There would be too many questions I didn't think I could answer. Hastily, I swept Violet into my arms and into my tiny cottage. Safely inside, I had her sit at my rickety kitchen table. I quickly changed my shirt, washed my face, and ran water through my hair. In the mirror, I saw Violet eyeing me inquisitively.

I turned around and she licked her lips.

"I'm so thirsty," Violet whimpered.

"I know," I said helplessly.

Just then, the cabin door creaked open. I glanced around in a panic. Perhaps my cabin wasn't as secluded as I needed it to be.

"Stefan, you're back!" Oliver came barreling inside, his tiny footsteps echoing on the floor. He threw his arms around my knees. "I thought I saw you. You came home early! Are we going hunting today?"

"Not yet," I said, ruffling his fine blond hair and trying to choke back my guilt. "I have a visitor. Oliver, this is Violet."

His eyes widened at the site of her, reminding me of the way Violet captivated the crowds at the theater. She did have something special about her.

"She's my cousin," I lied as Violet sank to her knees and held out her hand.

"Hello, little man," she said, giving Oliver a big smile.

But Oliver continued to stare at her, not moving a muscle. His face subtly changed from a sense of wonder to hesitation. Could he somehow sense her new nature? Back in Virginia, our horses would always become uneasy when Katherine was in their midst. But could the same apply to children?

"Is she going hunting with us?" Oliver asked, not taking his eyes off Violet.

"No, I'm sorry, she can't," I said briefly, hoping he wouldn't push for an explanation.

"Can you at least come to dinner? We've missed you, Stefan!"

"Yes. Why don't you run up and let Mrs. Duckworth know that Violet and I are here? We'll see you soon." Oliver nodded, but didn't move.

"Go on!" I urged. I hadn't wanted the Abbotts to meet Violet. I'd wanted her to die in peace. But I didn't want to arouse suspicion, and now we'd have to attend dinner and pretend that everything was in order. Already, Violet's skin had taken on a ghastly pallor, a clear indication that death was working its way through her body. Who knew how much worse she'd be in an hour? Time was of the essence, and I felt terrible that I was making her spend her last few hours living a lie.

"Yes, Stefan," Oliver said, trudging out the door and up the stone walk to the house.

"We have to go to dinner," I said. "I'm sorry."

"No, that's okay," Violet said. She looked drawn and overwhelmed, and guilt twisted in my stomach. Maybe she'd find some small comfort at the farmhouse. At least I could hope.

"I'm going to tell them that you're my second cousin," I explained as I led her up the winding path toward the large brick manor house. "We met in London and I invited you to the country for a few days. Does that sound okay?"

Violet nodded. She was still licking her lips and I couldn't help but notice how large her pupils were becoming. She was well into the transition, cresting to the peak where her very being was fighting to survive in any way possible, even if that meant drinking blood.

"Stefan!" George bellowed as we entered the foyer. It was clear Oliver had relayed my message, and he'd been expecting us. George's paunch was straining against his waistcoat, and his face was redder than ever. "You're here in time for dinner. And I was worried you'd be so caught up by the city that you'd never come back to the country. But

I see you came home! And with company!" he added, his gaze flicking curiously toward Violet.

"Sir," I said quickly, my stomach twisting on the word *home*. "I invited my cousin, Violet, to explore our town. I am sorry for the short notice."

"I heard so much about this place and I felt I had to come," Violet said, playing her part like the actress she was. She curtseyed prettily.

"Cousin Violet," George murmured. "Enchanted, my darling," he said, bowing slightly at her.

The three of us walked into the parlor. I could smell a roast being prepared in the kitchen, and I loved how familiar and simple my surroundings seemed. Luke and Oliver were on the floor, playing a game of dominos, Emma was rocking a doll in her arms, and Gertrude was working on her needlepoint, an exquisitely crafted flower scene. Nothing had changed here, and yet, for me, everything had.

"How was London?" George boomed, catching my eye as he crossed over to the drink cart in the corner and poured a dark amber liquid into two glasses.

"It was fine," I said shortly. "Loud."

"I can imagine. And where did you stay? With your relations, the—"

"Burnses," Violet said quickly. "I'm Violet Burns." I watched her. Were her eyes too bright, her face too pale? I couldn't tell.

"He wasn't too much trouble, was he?" George teased.

I grimaced internally. They had no idea that trouble followed me everywhere. "No, he was lovely," Violet said finally, as if she'd been coached.

A fond smile crossed George's face. "Our Stefan has that effect on people. And I'm so happy you have relations nearby. A man shouldn't have to fend for himself in the world," he said, catching my eye as he raised his glass in the air. "To family," he said, tipping it toward me.

"To family," I murmured, nursing my own drink. A silence fell in the room and I was all too relieved when Mrs. Duckworth came into the parlor to announce that the roast was ready.

Violet licked her lips as she stood up and smoothed her skirts. She'd been doing it obsessively, and my heart went out to her. I knew that she was experiencing her first pangs of real, soul-crushing hunger that couldn't be quenched with any mortal meal.

"Violet, darling, sit here," Gertrude said, guiding Violet to a seat next to her at the large cherrywood table. "You look half-starved, which is understandable. I'm sure the food they serve on those trains is appalling!" She clucked sympathetically.

"I'm sorry," Violet said distantly. "I don't feel very well."

"Well, have a bite to eat, and then if you need to have a lie down, go ahead and do it. A good meal, some country air, and you'll be good as new," Gertrude said in her loving, maternal way.

We settled, and I watched as Mrs. Duckworth cut the roast. A trickle of blood oozed from the meat with each cut, and I saw Violet lean forward, her blue eyes shining.

"Here you go, dear," Mrs. Duckworth said, putting two slices on her plate. Without waiting for the rest of the family to be served, or helping herself to the potatoes, beans, and rolls set in heaping bowls on the table, Violet dug in. She barely used her utensils as she shoveled the meat into her mouth.

"You *must* have been hungry," Gertrude trilled as she stood up to help Luke cut his meat. Luke, perhaps taking a cue from Violet, was forgoing his knife in favor of stabbing his slice of meat with his fork.

"I don't know what came over me," Violet said, dabbing her mouth with her napkin. Her gaze was still on the meat. A silence hung in the room.

"Just the brisk country air," Gertrude repeated, an edge to her voice. I knew that the Abbotts could sense something was wrong, but they couldn't put their fingers on it. I desperately wanted them to like her, and for Violet to find the same type of peace on the farm that I'd found. But of course, Violet felt confused and famished. Damon or not, maybe it would have been better if she'd died surrounded by the marquee lights of the West End.

"Have you always lived in London, dear?" Gertrude asked, obviously giving Violet the benefit of the doubt.

"I'm originally from Ireland," Violet said, her mouth full of food. Luke and Oliver were watching her with fascination.

"Ireland." George cleared his throat. "I thought your relations were from Italy, Stefan."

"They were on my father's side. There's some Irish blood on my mother's side," I lied. If Damon could reinvent himself as a count or a duke, I could invent some Irish relatives.

"Ah," George said, slicing into his own meat. "Well, in any case, it's lovely to have you here, Violet. Consider our house your house."

"You're too kind," Violet murmured, her eyes frantically darting around the table, desperately looking for something to satiate her hunger. Even though there was nothing that could.

Just then, Emma pulled timidly on the sleeve of Violet's dress.

Violet glanced down, her wary expression changing into a wide smile. "Why, hello there, little dear," Violet said gently.

"Hi," Emma said, immediately putting her thumb in her mouth and looking away.

"Now, Emma, can you properly introduce yourself to Miss Violet?"

I watched Emma nervously. I was still wary of the way Oliver had stared at Violet. Was something apparent about Violet to the children that wasn't to their parents?

"I'm Emma," she said solemnly, before sticking her thumb back in her mouth.

Violet smiled, suddenly looking much stronger than she had before.

"Hello, Emma. I'm Violet. And you're *very* pretty. When I first saw you, do you know what I thought?"

"No." Emma shook her head.

"I thought, that girl must be a fairy princess. There's no way she could be a human. She's far too lovely. Are you a princess?" Violet asked.

Without saying anything, Emma clambered up on Violet's lap. Violet bounced her up and down on her knee.

"I think you found a new friend," Gertrude said, clearly charmed by Emma's worship of Violet.

"I think I have, too, and I'm most thankful for it," Violet said, her eyes shining. "I have a sister about her age back home; her name is Clare. I miss her very much. And then of course I have another sister, Cora. She's in London," Violet said, her eyes taking on a longing expression.

"It must be hard to be so far away. What brought you to London?" George asked. Emma's fondness had broken any ice, and now the Abbotts were behaving as if Violet was just one more slightly older member of their brood.

"Well, I thought I'd be an actress," Violet admitted.

"Well, you still can. You're how old? Seventeen?" Gertrude asked as she patted the corner of her mouth with her white linen napkin.

Violet nodded. "Yes, I suppose I could be," she said, sighing. Through the entire conversation, she'd been eating ravenously, almost faster than Mrs. Duckworth could refill her plate. Luke and Oliver were watching in admiration, clearly in awe of her appetite. After all, they'd often tried to have eating competitions in the past, only to be admonished by Mrs. Duckworth with a sharp rap to their knuckles.

"Well, Stefan, your family is lovely, just like I'd imagine. It's as my husband said, family truly is the most important thing in life," Gertrude said, her intelligent blue eyes shining.

"I agree," I said thickly.

Violet finally put down her fork and slumped over, resting her elbows on the table. Her eyes were glassy and her face was ghostly white.

"Are you all right, dear?" Gertrude asked, pushing back her chair. Hurriedly, Mrs. Duckworth raced over to assist her.

"She's fine. She's just had a long day. We left London quite early," I said frantically, wondering if this was the beginning of the end.

"Of course. Well, I can have the guest room prepared if . . ."

Violet sat up and took a few deep breaths. Aware all eyes were on her, she smoothed back her auburn hair and sat ramrod straight. Her smile was frozen into a grimace. It all must have been excruciating to her. "I apologize. I'm quite all right, thank you," she said, her voice strong and steady.

I placed my own napkin next to my plate and stood up to help Violet. She needed to be alone, and quickly.

"I think we'll go for a walk. As you said, the air will do us good," I said, pulling Violet's chair back and offering her my arm. She was about to die, and I couldn't have that happen in the Manor. I'd come up with something to tell the Abbotts later—that she'd decided to head back to London to see her doctor, and that she sent her regards. After twenty years of lying, I'd learned to think of all the eventualities.

Oliver stirred impatiently at the end of the table. "Can we go hunting? Please? I've been practicing all day and you promised. Violet can come with us!"

"Oliver!" Gertrude admonished. "Stefan will be entertaining his cousin."

"Another time, Oliver," I said, patting his head. "Just keep working on your aim and you'll be able to teach me something when we go out," I said. Violet smiled slightly, and I felt another heavy dose of regret. Accident or not, I'd led her to Damon. Because of me, Violet would never have a family of her own. "Thank you very much for a lovely meal," I said. I held my hand out for Violet and the two of us walked into the afternoon light.

There was a chill in the air, and I realized how close we were to fall. The longer I lived, the more I became aware of how quickly the seasons changed. Sometimes I felt like one had barely begun before we were on to the next—so unlike when I was a human, when a summer seemed to stretch for a lifetime. It was just one of the millions of tiny losses that I endured, that Violet wouldn't have to.

"I don't know what came over me at dinner," Violet confessed as I led her up the rock-strewn path through the glen. I thought it would be nice to head to Ivinghoe Beacon. It was the tallest spot in the parish, taller even than the large waterwheel that churned in the Chiltern River to power the mines down below.

We walked companionably through the glittering green glen, which seemed more alive than ever. Sparrows chirped, chipmunks and squirrels rattled in the dense shrubbery, and I could hear the sound of the brook rushing toward Bilbury Creek.

Violet stopped mid-step.

"Are you all right?" I asked delicately. It seemed a terrible question to ask. Of course she wasn't all right.

Violet shook her head. "I'll miss everything," she said,

spreading her hands wide as if to take the whole view in. I saw her shoulders rise and fall, heard a slight gasp escape her lips. But she didn't cry.

I grabbed her hand. There was nothing I could say, so we continued walking up the hill, until the grass turned rougher, the rocks larger, and the air slightly thinner. We walked through a dense forest of evergreen trees until the moment I was waiting for—when the trees cleared and all that was left was blue sky above, and England sprawling down below. It was one of my favorite spots in the world, second only to the far edge of the property of my child-hood home in Virginia where the pond met the forest.

"Thank you for taking me here," she said finally. She put her hand on her heart. "Oh, *Stefan*!" she called out in anguish.

"Shhh," I said, pulling her close. I wasn't sure how else I could comfort her. Around us, birds continued to chirp and the autumn air ruffled her skirts. But inside, I knew she was weakening. "Shhh," I said again.

She buried her face in her hands against my chest. I held her as she sobbed, each shudder of hers a twist in my heart. Finally, she pried her fingers off and looked at me with such a piercing gaze that I stepped back.

"Why me?" she asked, her eyes searching my face.

"It's my fault. If you hadn't met me, this never would have happened," I said miserably.

Violet shook her head. "Or maybe I'd be dead in a London ditch. You were my friend. You showed me the world. If I have to die, at least I had those days of magic," she said shyly.

"Thank you," I said. I thought back to when we met. There was no way I would have ever forgiven myself if I'd just walked away when Alfred yelled at her in the tavern. "That's very kind. But please know I only did what anyone would do, Violet."

"I don't believe that," she said firmly. "You're a true friend."

"And you are, too. I'll always remember you."

A slow smile crossed Violet's face. "You'll always remember me? Even in two hundred years?"

"Yes," I replied. I had no doubt. I wanted good memories of Violet, wanted to remember the courageous resolve she'd shown even in the face of her own death. "You're one in a million. And you're someone I could never, ever forget."

Gratitude gleamed in Violet's eyes. "Thank you," she said in a small voice. "May I ask you a favor?"

I nodded. I knew if I spoke, my voice would crack, and I didn't want to cry in front of Violet. I didn't want her to know how terrified I was.

"Could you . . . kiss me?" she whispered, embarrassed. "It's just that I've never had a proper kiss. And I don't want to die without ever being kissed. Please?"

Once again, I found my heart breaking for this girl. She had so much life left to live. I nodded, grasping her tiny, delicate hand and pulling her into me. I leaned down and allowed my lips to graze hers in a sweet, innocent kiss.

Violet broke the kiss and shyly met my gaze.

"Thank you," she said. "That was perfect."

"Don't thank me," I mumbled. In that moment, I felt something as close to peace as I'd felt in years.

I glanced at the sky to avoid looking at her. Clouds were rolling in toward the river down below, and I knew it would only be a matter of time before the heavens opened up.

I hurried Violet down the hill without a backward glance. The rain would come soon, causing the grounds to sparkle with condensation. I loved rainstorms, their ability to wash everything away and make everything smell clean and innocent. I only wished the rain could wash away my sins.

16

When I was growing up, kissing was a game that we started to play when we found tag to be too childlike. It was a diversion, an amusement, and caused our hearts to race at an otherwise boring picnic. I'd shared kisses with Clementine Haverford, Amelia Hawke, Rosalyn Cartwright, and all my other childhood playmates. Kissing was pleasant, but never life-changing.

But then, I kissed Katherine Pierce, and nothing was ever the same. It was as if those other kisses were mere shadows of the ecstasy I felt when Katherine's lips were near mine. When I was surrounded by her heady scent of lemon and ginger, I was guided purely by instinct. I would do anything for a kiss.

*And, of course, it was that unquenchable desire
that had changed my entire life. Katherine was like
Helen of Troy, launching an eternity of destruction. And yet, I knew that if I ever did find myself
close to death, I would close my eyes and imagine
Katherine's lips brushing mine.*

*Violet wanted something I couldn't give her.
She wanted love, and all I had was my affection.
But maybe that was better than desire. Desire,
after all, was the very thing that killed me.*

In autumn, thick rain clouds often hung low in the
Ivinghoe sky, casting the entire farm in a gloomy, dusklike
fog no matter what the time of day. Today was no excep-
tion. The beautiful morning had given way to an evening
heavy with the promise of rain and in the semidarkness of
my cabin, I was watching Violet grow weaker and weaker.
Here, it was just us and Death, a powerful third party in
my vigil over Violet.

"Please, Stefan!" Violet said, thrashing from side to side
as she woke. I hastily dipped a compress in water and held
it against her forehead. My knees were stiff, and I knew I
must have been sitting in the same position for hours, but I
didn't want to leave her side for even an instant. I couldn't
tell whether her screams were the result of a fever dream or
a sign that she was returning to a hazy half-consciousness.

Violet's eyes, when they opened, were cloudy as unshaken milk. She squinted, trying to focus on me.

"Stefan, please! Please just kill me. End it now," she gasped, her breathing sounding like a rusty saw cutting against metal. Whitish froth had collected at the corners of her mouth and her arms were covered with scratches from when she'd clawed at her skin in her sleep, as if wanting to escape her own body. I'd stopped her as best I could, but she still looked like she'd run through a bramble patch. Now, she no longer had energy to thrash, and all she could focus on was blinking and breathing.

I shook my head dully. I wished I could do what she asked of me—to end her agony and bring her peace. But no matter how much she begged, I couldn't bring myself to do it. I'd promised to myself over and over again that I'd never kill another human. It was selfish, perhaps, but all I could do was try to make her comfortable in her last moments.

"Please!" she cried, her voice a half-shriek. An owl hooted in the distance. Nighttime was when the creatures of the forest came out. I could smell their blood and hear their heartbeats. And while Violet couldn't hear them as profoundly as I did, I knew she could sense their presence as well.

"Soon you'll be somewhere better," I said, hoping upon hope that I was telling her the truth. "Soon you'll be at peace. And it will be better than here or London—better than Ireland, even. It will be better than anywhere you or I could imagine."

"Stefan, it hurts," Violet said, thrashing against the bed frame and throwing the bedclothes on the floor. She opened her eyes again.

"Shhh—" I said, reaching toward her arm. But she yanked away from me, swung her feet down, and raced toward the door, a tangle of bedclothes mopping the floor behind her.

"Violet!" I sprang up, my chair falling behind me with a clatter. Quickly, Violet loosened the latch and fled into the night. The door slammed shut.

I immediately ran after her. I looked this way and that, my senses quickly acclimating to the outdoors. The air was pitch black, and the trees surrounding the cottage, usually so cozy, made me realize she could be anywhere.

I sniffed the air, suddenly sharp with the smell of blood, and raced toward the source.

"Violet!" I called into the night, aware and not caring that the Abbotts could hear me. I needed to find her. I hopped over the wire fence of the chicken coop.

There, kneeling, her dress, face, and hands spattered with blood, was Violet. A dead chicken was in her lap, its neck snapped, blood oozing from a gash on its throat. Blood was running down Violet's face, and her teeth, still normal, gleamed in the moonlight.

Suddenly, she leaned over and began to retch. Her entire body was soaked in sweat, and I couldn't tell if she was dying or reviving.

"I'm so sorry!" she said, her face stained with tears. "I didn't mean to do it."

Violet's guilt was one I knew all too well. Wordlessly, I took her by the hand, pulled her up, and led her back to the cabin. I closed the door and turned toward her. Her body was perched on the edge of the bed, bloodstains in her hair and on the bodice of her dress, her expression miserable.

"Are you mad at me?" she asked in a tiny voice.

I shook my head silently and helped her lie down, tucking her under the crisp white linen sheets and opening the window, hoping that the fall air could provide some solace.

"I was so hungry," she said in a small voice. "I still am."

"I know," I said. The chicken blood wouldn't do anything. To turn, a vampire needed human blood. "I know it's hard. And I know you're suffering," I said helplessly. She nodded, a drop of chicken blood still lingering on the corner of her mouth. "But remember, you're going someplace better. I truly believe that. And I know it will be painful, but after pain comes peace."

I suppose I also hoped that for my sake as well. After all, I had created this. My mind kept playing the same tug-of-war over and over again. The logical part of my brain told me that this could have happened whether or not I'd been involved. After all, if Violet and I had never met, she might have been kicked out to the street. She could have been found by anyone.

Or she might be on the brink of a long, happy life.

"Stefan, I . . ." Violet said, breathing heavily with every word.

"It's all right. Go and find peace," I said. It was the good-bye I'd never given Callie. Now, I knew that the best thing I could do was let Violet know it was okay to go.

"But . . . I . . ." Violet said, her breath laboring with each word. I leaned in closer to hear, my ear just inches away from her mouth, when all of a sudden, I heard a terrible, otherworldly shriek piercing the night air.

But it wasn't Violet. It was coming from the Manor.

I tore my gaze away from Violet and rushed up to the house, fearing the worst.

he Manor was pitch-black, and there was no sign of anyone, not even Mrs. Duckworth, who often kept late hours knitting by candlelight. There wasn't even a lantern lighting the porch, and I felt my stomach sink. Something was very, very wrong.

"Hello?" I called, my voice wavering. "Who's here?" I called again, wishing I'd remembered to grab a gun before I'd run to the house. "Show yourself!" I yelled, louder than ever, my voice echoing off the stone entranceway.

Silence. Damon must have found us.

Then, I heard a slight cry. It was so faint, I thought I might be imagining things. I cocked my head again. Definitely a noise.

"I'm coming!" I called. If there was sound, it was a sign of life. I quickly sped through the labyrinth of rooms, my eyes adjusting to the dim light, until I came into the parlor.

There, the entire Abbott family was huddled in the corner, Luke as white as a ghost. George was clutching a poker, his eyes wild, and Gertrude had fainted on the floor. Emma, the source of the noise, was crying over her mother. But they were alive.

"I'm here. It's Stefan. You're safe," I said to the family, even though my heart was pounding in terror against my chest. Damon could be anywhere. He was probably right behind me, laughing at me. He'd concocted this scene purely to frighten me, to show me that he wasn't scared of Klaus because he'd *become* Klaus. He could commit horrific acts of bloodshed without blinking an eye.

"Stefan?" George said incredulously, his voice dripping with fear.

"Yes. You'll be safe. I promise," I said, my eyes darting around the room. The many portraits seemed to be leering down at me. But there was no sign of Damon.

Suddenly, I heard a noise and whirled around. As soon as my back was turned, George sprang up, lunging toward me with the poker. A crazed look was on his florid face.

"Traitor! You stole my son!" George yelled, swinging the iron poker wildly through the air as if it were a sword. I ducked easily, horror dawning on me as I took in the family. *Where was Oliver?*

"Sir! No! I was down at the farmhouse! It was my brother, *Damon*. Where is he? Did you see where he went?" I asked desperately as I continued to duck his blows.

I felt something jump on my back. I spun around and realized Luke had clamped himself to my shoulders and was kicking his legs into my lungs.

"You took my brother!" he shrieked, pummeling his feet into my back. I struggled against his grip. Emma was crying loudly now, tears streaming down her face.

"Fiend! You shall die!" George roared, lunging toward me in the darkness.

"It wasn't me!" I yelled futilely. I shrugged Luke off my back. He fell to the floor with a sickening *thump*, and I used the moment George turned to tend to him to hurry out of the house and into the darkness, confident my vampire senses would give me a head start. But I knew I didn't have much time. George would run to a neighboring farm for help, and soon there'd be an entire mob looking for me.

But right now, I couldn't worry about that. Oliver was kidnapped. And a vampire was on the loose. I'd been set up, just like I had when Martha had been found in the alley behind the Ten Bells. Fear flooded my body as I realized the connection. Oliver had been taken for a reason, and I'd left Violet unattended and vulnerable. He was going to get to her and force the choice she'd fought so hard against.

Oliver would be the sacrificial lamb. I was just a pawn in my brother's game, and this time, he was truly playing for blood.

"Damon!" I yelled again into the darkness. I sniffed the air, feeling the urge to retch when I smelled the familiar iron scent all around, enveloping me. "Damon!" My feet flew toward my cabin, and I pushed against the door with all my might.

I blinked in horror.

In the center of the floor was Violet, leaning down over Oliver, taking large sips from a gaping wound on his neck. Blood was trickling onto the floor in a dark, deep pool.

"Oliver!" I called helplessly. Violet turned around, her newly formed fangs glistening with blood, a blank expression on her face. She leaned down, burying her face back in Oliver's neck.

"No!" I lunged toward them and attempted to grab Oliver from her grasp. The little boy's body was limp and lifeless, and I couldn't hear a heartbeat. But his tiny body wasn't entirely drained of blood. Not yet. Violet pulled him away from my hands and brought his neck to her lips.

Just then, I heard the door click shut. I turned, ready to fight my brother.

Only it wasn't Damon. Framed in the doorway was Samuel, his hair blond and lionlike around his face, his white shirt and tan trousers impeccably pressed. I blinked. So Samuel was one of Damon's foot soldiers as well. Of course. I felt the hatred for my brother deepening.

"Where is he?" I growled, my hands flexing into fists. I would make Samuel pay, but first, I needed him to lead me to Damon.

"So this is your country estate, Stefan," Samuel said, unwinding his bow tie and draping it over the back of a chair and sitting down as if he were paying a simple social call.

"Where's Damon?" I repeated.

"I don't know." Samuel shrugged, crossing one leg over his knee and leaning back on his chair. "And I don't care. I came here looking for you. Our time in London was so rushed, I felt that you hardly got to know me at all," he said, arching a blond eyebrow.

"You're not here for Damon?"

"Your brother?" he asked lazily, licking his lips. "Not hardly. As I said, I have no idea where he is. Nor do I care. What really matters is where people *think* Damon is," Samuel said, a small smile playing on his lips.

"What do you mean?" I asked, my head spinning. I couldn't stop staring at the stone on his necklace, and the more I stared at it, the more bewitched I felt by it.

"I mean that Damon . . . or, I'm sorry, *Count DeSangue*, may soon have another soubriquet. I hope he likes the sound of 'Jack the Ripper.'" Samuel rose and stalked toward Violet, who was still crouched over Oliver. She seemed unsure whether to dive back in and feed again. Samuel stood above them, and for a second, I wondered if Samuel would snap Violet's neck, too, simply to show his power. But he didn't. Instead, his hand rested gently on the top of Violet's head.

"I think you could be useful," he mused to himself. "Yes, I think you have what it takes. Hunger, certainly," he said as Violet lowered her head to drink as if in a trance. Then he turned toward me.

"Where's Damon?" I asked, my voice shaking. "Is he . . ."

"Dead?" Samuel let out a harsh laugh that sounded like a bark. "What would possibly be the fun in that? I can promise you, he's not dead. I came up with another plan for him. Since I know how much he craves the spotlight, I found a way for him to be splashed all over the London papers. He's about to be known as London's most notorious killer. They're receiving an eyewitness sketch of him as we speak. And that's just the beginning. I think he'll like that, don't you?"

"You're the Ripper," I realized, everything clicking into place. Samuel had murdered Mary Ann and attacked Martha. And Samuel intended to frame Damon for the murders. Which meant that *Samuel* had written the warning message in the park.

I stepped back, my body slamming against the wall. I'd cornered myself.

"I want to destroy Damon. And death would be far too easy," Samuel hissed, stepping up to me and laying one hand on each shoulder. "So I will make him pay first. I'll take him away from the London society he loves so much and ruin the image he enjoys maintaining. That was the plan, and that's what shall be carried out," Samuel explained, his face now inches away from mine. "When you came along, I didn't have quite as much time to plot your punishment. But I'm quite pleased by what I came up with. I ruined the family you loved so much and blamed it on you. I got your girl to come to the dark side . . . I think I did rather well," Samuel said, smiling.

"Why are you doing this to us? What have we ever done to you?" I asked, trying to placate him by not struggling. My mind was whirling. I could just hear the sound of shouting in the distance, and knew it wouldn't be long before an angry mob surrounded the cabin.

"You did enough. And I don't really feel like giving you a history lesson. But speaking of brothers, I do know that you hurt mine. And I think that alone makes a rather strong case against us being friends, don't you agree?" he asked. His smile was dangerous, and I knew he was about to pounce. I closed my eyes, gathered my strength, and charged toward him, hoping the surprise of my action would catch him off guard.

But quicker than lightning, he wrestled me to the ground until I was pinned underneath him. With his face only inches from mine, I could smell human blood on his breath.

I twisted free and scrambled backward. He seemed to be everywhere and nowhere all at once, and suddenly, I caught the whiff of something burning. Our scuffle had upset a table, and an overturned candle had started a fire, the flames licking the dry pine walls. The light from the flames danced on Samuel's angular face. Our eyes locked for a moment, and a faint smile crossed Samuel's lips. Then he lunged toward me, catching me unaware as he pushed me toward the hearth. I fell onto my knees.

"Get out," Samuel barked to Violet, who ran toward the door, leaving Oliver's lifeless body on the ground.

"You've lived for far too long," he said, quickly grabbing a chair and snapping it over his knee as if it were a twig. He stood over me, each foot on either side of my waist, one hand holding a broken chair limb, ready for it to serve as a stake.

But instead of driving it into my chest, he glanced at me in disgust, then spit onto my face.

"You're not worth killing; that's too easy," Samuel muttered, almost to himself. "I want you to suffer. You deserve it. In fact, that's the only thing you deserve."

I closed my eyes, not bothering to fight. Instead, I allowed my mind to conjure up Callie. Sweet, fierce Callie, with red hair and freckled skin and mischievous eyes. I knew this would be the last time I saw her, even in my imagination. She was surely in heaven, and I would soon be bound for hell.

With Samuel's swift motion, pain was everywhere. The stake had driven through my chest, but missed my heart. Pain radiated from the wound to my hands, my feet, my brain.

"Enjoy hell," Samuel said with a laugh. Then he swept out the door, leaving me in the fire-filled cabin, a precursor to what I knew was to be my final resting place.

hen death is inevitable, the passage of time both quickens and slows. It had happened the first time I died, when I felt a bullet rip through my body, and I felt it now. I felt the heat from the flames that raced along the perimeter of the cabin. I felt pain pulsing in my gut. I felt trapped, unable to wiggle the stake more than a few inches in any direction. But what I also felt was regret, anger, sorrow, and relief. It truly was as if a lifetime were passing before my eyes.

Or rather, both my lifetimes.

I hadn't accomplished very much, either as a human or a vampire. What I'd accomplished was death. And as much as I felt I was better than Damon, was I, really? For in the end, we were both vampires. We both had a trail of destruction following us. And I was so tired. I was tired of fighting when nothing seemed to work out. I was tired of hurting. And I was tired of always being a puppet in Damon's games. We were no longer children, the games had been deadly for far too long, and maybe my death was the only thing that would end our war. If so, I embraced it. I was ready to be consumed by an eternity of flames. That would be more peaceful than the life I'd been living.

The fire was taking its time, dancing along the seam between the wall and floorboards as if it were a cautious beau at a ball. I watched, entranced. The flames were made up of red and blue and orange and, from a distance, they reminded me of the brilliant fall leaves that would soon dot Abbott Manor. I'd never see that again.

Please don't kill them, I thought, thinking of the rest of the Abbott family, frightened, grieving, and so terribly, terribly betrayed. It was a habit, thinking others could read my thoughts. It had sometimes worked with Damon and me, but that had only been because our closeness as brothers meant we often could guess what was on each others' minds. I doubted Samuel and I were on any sort of familiar wavelength that would allow him to receive a message like that from me. Not that it mattered. Hearing it would only further encourage his thirst for blood.

I didn't care about my own life, but I felt a tiny tug of loyalty toward Violet, who was now off with Samuel somewhere. She was a brand-new vampire, surely confused and overwhelmed. She needed guidance. And not the kind a cold-hearted killer would give her.

I tried to move my arm, desperate to pull the stake out. A renewed vigor surged through my limbs. I wasn't ready to die. Not until I could save Violet from becoming a monster. I owed her that much after she was denied her choice. I tried to tear the stake from my chest as flames came closer and closer to my body. I heard the sound of the door creak, and I arched into the pain, ready to confront my fate.

"He's in here!" It was a girl's voice.

My eyes snapped open and I saw Violet's sister, Cora, her red hair flaming around her face and dark circles under her eyes. Her pendant swung back and forth from her chest, momentarily mesmerizing me. I closed my eyes again. Just one more person I probably couldn't save. When I was desperate to get Violet out of Damon's clutches, I had abandoned Cora.

"I'm sorry," I whispered to the dream-image.

But then, I felt lightness in my chest, from where the chair leg had been. My eyes flew open.

"You almost got yourself killed, brother," Damon said. Before I even fully comprehended what was happening, I felt warm liquid rushing down my throat. I gagged as I realized a red fur carcass was being shoved into my face.

It was the limp body of a fox.

"Drink more," Damon instructed impatiently, glancing nervously behind his back. The flames were higher now, having caught onto the wall.

"What are you doing here?" I asked as more blood trickled down my throat.

"Saving your life," Damon said, dragging me to my feet and pulling me outside and into the forest, just as my tiny cabin exploded into flames behind us. "After you left the party I realized Samuel was the one who must have killed Violet," Damon continued. "The blood under his fingernails practically gleamed against his champagne glass. When I confronted him about it, he said he had a plan in motion, for both of us, and he took off. Let's just say I decided to not let you die, at least not today. You can thank me later," Damon said, brusquely depositing me on the cool forest floor. Far in the distance, I heard a cacophony of bells, screams, and thudding horse hooves. It was just like the siege Father had begun in Virginia. And once again, my brother and I were side by side, sticking together.

"We have to run!" I said raggedly. "Turn left." We didn't have time for a long explanation, but if Damon could have some compassion in him, I thought we could escape anything. I knew the forest better than anyone, and once we got to the center, underneath trees so tall the sky wasn't visible even on a clear summer day, we'd be all right.

Damon picked Cora up and threw her over his shoulder with one hand while half-dragging me with another. We ran over the brook and around a quarry, circling the far perimeter of the Abbott farm, and finally, I brought them to the glen below the Chiltern River. It was a place that would take humans half a day to reach, but with us running at vampire speed, we had reached it in no time. We were safe. At least for now.

"I'm going to find Samuel," Damon said, his face red from exertion. "He needs to know the consequences of his actions."

"Damon, do you know what he's done? He's framed you for the Jack the Ripper murders. The police are getting a sketch of you even now. You can't follow him; it's not safe," I said.

"I won't let him get away with this, brother," Damon said angrily. "Stay here. I'm going to see if I can find him."

I didn't have the strength to argue with him. I could hardly believe I was alive. I sat down on a rock and cradled my head in my hands. Then I held my hand over my wound. It was shrinking, but it still hurt, and I felt like there was a tiny heart beating in time to my breath.

"Are you all right?" Cora asked finally, breaking the silence. She was sitting on a fallen tree branch opposite me, nervously biting her fingernails. I wondered how much she knew about Damon's true nature. But I had no energy to ask questions. I sank back upon the leaves as Cora sat beside me, eyeing me like a hawk. I could hear her heart thumping—*ba-dump, ba-dump*—and I sighed in relief. If I could hear her heart, that meant she hadn't turned. She was human. I concentrated on the noise, as reassuring as the raindrops during an April shower.

I had to tell her about her sister.

"Violet . . ." I began.

"How is she?"

I shook my head. "Not well," I managed to say. Cora's heart sped up, but her breathing continued to be steady.

"Is she a vampire?" Cora asked, locking eyes with me. I couldn't lie.

"Yes, she turned," I said. "Samuel forced her."

A flash of hope lit up Cora's eyes. "She did? So she's not dead. Well, not *dead* dead. But . . . where did she go?" she asked in confusion.

"Samuel took her," I said. "She didn't have a choice. She must be frightened."

"I'm sure she is," Cora said in a small voice, twisting her vervain charm around her index finger. "When we were children, Violet used to have to fall asleep with a candle burning all night. She was always afraid of monsters coming to get her."

"She'll get over that soon enough," I said wryly. As a vampire, the dark was soon to become Violet's biggest comfort.

"I suppose so," Cora said, staring into space.

"Are you all right?" I asked.

Cora shrugged. "I hardly know. I was at the party, and Samuel came up to me, and I started shrieking. I didn't know where the sound had come from. I didn't even know that it was me. But he terrified me. And then your brother found me and made me talk. He brought me on the train. I kept praying Violet would be all right, but . . . could she be all right?" she said in a small voice.

I nodded. I didn't want to give her false hope. "She'll be different. But I can teach her. There are things that make being a vampire less terrible," I said.

"Good." We lapsed into silence. The wound in my chest was shrinking, and far above us I saw the faintest signs of dawn breaking through the inky night. I'd be all right. I'd live to see another day, another decade, another century. But Oliver wouldn't. And where was Damon?

"Damon's taking a long time," Cora said, echoing my own thoughts. "Do you think he'll be safe?"

"Yes," I said. In truth, I didn't know. I was only beginning to become aware of the different and vast expanse of vampires living in the world. Before, I'd thought I only needed to concern myself with Originals, like Klaus. But there were so many others to be worried about, in ways I'd never considered. "Damon's very good at looking after himself," I said.

A silence fell between us.

Suddenly, I heard a rustle in the woods. I stiffened as the footsteps drew closer, and conversation carried through the trees.

"Anything, men? Nothing over in those bushes?"

I heard the loud barking of several dogs. Footsteps passed nearby and I pushed my back against the rough bark of a tree. Cora squeezed my hand tightly until the group left, spurred on by the manic barking of the dogs.

"They're looking for me," I said, dully stating the obvious after the last footsteps had long since passed.

"Well, they didn't find you, did they? That's good news," Cora said in her lilting brogue, attempting a watery smile.

I smiled back. It wasn't much, but it was true. They hadn't found us. Maybe I needed to learn to be thankful for small miracles.

Finally, as the sun's early rays fell on us, Damon broke through the brush, Oliver's lifeless body in his arms. His face was drawn and a jagged stream of blood trickled from his temple. He was shoeless, his clothes were torn, and he looked nothing like an Italian count or British merchant. Instead, he looked like the Damon of our childhood who'd spend hours playing in the woods. Except this was a game of life and death.

"I couldn't find Samuel," Damon said, sinking to a rock and sighing. "I tried to revive the child, but I couldn't."

"I know," I said, picking up Oliver's lifeless body. I'd never taken him hunting. I walked a few paces away, toward a grove of oak trees. I glanced at the dark sky, praying for Oliver's salvation.

I tenderly laid the body on the forest floor and went to work creating a small, shallow grave. Then, I placed Oliver inside.

"Here lies the best hunter in Britain," I said, a tear threatening my eye. I dropped a few handfuls of dirt inside, and covered that with tree branches. I turned away, not able to look at the grave anymore, and walked toward Cora and Damon, huddled a few feet away.

"What about my sister?" I heard Cora whisper. I saw Damon shrug. I wondered if there was more to the story than he was telling. But I wasn't ready to hear it. Not yet.

I lay down on the hard forest floor a few yards away and closed my eyes, allowing sleep to overtake me. Even as my mind drifted toward unconsciousness, I knew the sleep would be rough and raw. But I deserved it. I deserved everything that was coming to me.

19

Ⅰ rolled around on the hard ground, desperately trying to find a comfortable place to sleep. But I couldn't. Every inch of my body hurt, as though hot pokers were sticking into my skin. My mouth tasted like sandpaper, and my limbs felt like lead.

In my half-conscious state, I didn't know where I was, but I had the familiar feeling I'd been here before. But where? If I was in hell, at least it was quiet. But then I blinked, and noticed two points of light moving toward me.

"Well, hello there," a voice said. I blinked again, and realized the two points of light were coming from two large, inquisitive eyes.

"Katherine," I croaked.

"Why, yes," she said, as though we were meeting each other on the dust-covered dirt road to Veritas Estate.

"This is a dream," I said, more to myself than to her.

"It could be," she said, her tone of voice light, as if I'd asked if she thought it might rain later that day. "But does it matter? We're both here."

"Why is this happening?"

"Some people can't let go. It can be difficult, can't it?" Katherine asked rhetorically.

I glanced at her eyes. They were wide, catlike, and more beautiful than ever. I remembered the hours I spent staring into them, back when I was willing to risk it all for her. And I had. I'd lost everything. But still, those eyes reminded me of what it felt like to be young and believe that love conquered all.

I wanted to ask her why she'd turned me, when she must have known that my life would be filled with sorrow. I wanted to know how she stood it. I wanted to know what I was supposed to do, now that I had lost everyone I cared about. And I wanted to know why she continued to haunt me.

"Scholarly Stefan," Katherine said, a smile playing on her lips. "Always thinking too hard. But remember, some things can't be understood or explained. They have to be experienced."

"Why?" I shouted, but Katherine simply faded into the darkness.

"We need to go," Damon said brusquely, poking my ribs with the tip of his boot.

"Now?" I struggled to my elbows before wiping sleep from my eyes. I knew from the dew on the ground that it was only a matter of time before the sky fully burst into morning.

Damon nodded. Cora stood a few paces away, her brow furrowed and arms crossed as she silently studied us.

"We're going back to London," Damon said firmly. "I need to find Samuel and teach him a lesson. No one bests Damon Salvatore. I'm going to beat him at his own game."

"We can't go back to London," I said, my jaw clenched as I rose to my full height, standing eye to eye with my brother. "Don't you see that? We need to stop fighting. You used to hate me; now you hate Samuel. It'll just lead to more bloodshed. Don't you understand?"

"Oh, I understand, brother. I understand you'd rather get yourself killed than say thanks to the brother who saved your life. I'm going to London. If you want to live in darkness and survive on sheep and rabbits, go ahead."

"I'm going, too. I have to find Violet," Cora said, her face pale and drawn. A glance passed between Cora and Damon, but I had no idea what it meant. Finally, Damon nodded.

"I'll come," I said. It wasn't as if I could stay here. Violet was out on her own, and I had to do everything I could to honor her dying wish. I couldn't let her become a monster. And Damon needed me, whether he knew it or not. And right now, when I had no one and no home, as much as I hated to admit it, I needed him.

I took off, leading the way through the forest to the train station. In the distance, I could hear a whistle. Freedom was only a few paces away. I sped up.

"And this time, no excuses for who you are, Stefan," Damon said, catching up to me, Cora on his back. "You're a vampire. When will you realize that?"

"I know who I am, Damon," I said calmly. It was a variation of the same argument we always had, but this time, I wasn't going to fight. I could see the train chugging into the station. We had to be careful. I was sure the entire parish was looking for us, and if we weren't ready to compel at a moment's notice, we could be caught unaware. "I'm your brother."

"Yes," Damon said after a beat.

It wasn't anywhere close to an apology, but I sensed something between us shift. If we wanted to find Samuel, we needed to work together. Maybe fighting Samuel was our only chance to stop the bloodshed that followed us. I had to believe it. I had to believe in something.

"Did you know that Samuel was a vampire?" I asked. It was a small question, but one I'd wondered in my feverish sleep. Had Damon voluntarily found a vampire society in London?

"No, I didn't know." Damon shook his head, his dark

eyes glinting in anger. "But I do know that I will never be made a fool of again. And I also know that Samuel's about to get a lesson he'll never forget."

"What if he's an Original?" I asked, my voice dropping to a whisper.

I cast my eyes to the sky, hoping that if there was light and goodness anywhere in the world, that Oliver was somewhere safe, in a place where he could do all the hunting he wanted.

"'What if he's an Original?'" Damon mocked, pulling me out of my reverie. "What does it matter? The only thing that matters is strength and determination. The Salvatore way," he said, his voice dripping with sarcasm. "Ready?" he asked, turning to Cora with a hint of a spark in his eye. With Damon, it was impossible to tell what he was thinking.

"All aboard!" the conductor said, waving us on. I tried not to imagine what he must think of the three of us: Damon with his ripped shirt; me with my chest wound oozing through my shirt; and Cora, still wearing her ever-present scarf tied in a dainty bow around her neck, despite her bloodstained bodice.

"Tickets?" the conductor asked suspiciously.

Damon smiled, his shoulders relaxing, clearly in his element.

"London. You've already seen our tickets, so you'll escort us to a first-class cabin. We won't see you for the rest of the trip. As far as you or anyone else is concerned, we're not there."

"Yes, sir, of course," the conductor said, nodding and ushering us through a narrow path onto the train.

I stared out the window as the verdant greenery rushed by. I wondered what was waiting for us in London. Would Samuel go on another killing spree? Did Violet really go with him willingly, or had she simply been bewildered after her transformation? And could Damon and I ever really work together?

All I knew was we were two revenge-seeking vampires, and we were about to bring on Samuel's destruction—no matter what the cost might be.

Twenty years ago—almost a lifetime ago—my brother and I escaped Mystic Falls on a train headed for New Orleans. We were baby vampires ourselves then. Damon was confused and searching, and I was blood-drunk and ready for action.

Now our roles had reversed. And yet, whether bound by a shared history or loyalty or even by blood—that mysterious, vexing, life-giving substance—we were together.

We didn't trust each other. We didn't like each other. But we were each other, reflecting our shadow, secret selves in the other's identity. We were running from a small-town mob that was after me, toward an entire city that believed

Damon to be the deadliest murderer in history. We were in it together.

And we deserved each other.

As much as I tried to hide it, I had a deadly dark side. And I saw, in Damon's concerned glances toward Cora and the gentle way he'd cradled Oliver's body as he brought him to me for burial, that Damon had a deeply feeling, human side. But could the two ever exist in tandem? And how many more humans would be killed before we could live in peace as vampires?

I didn't know the answer. But I knew there would be many more deaths. All I could hope was that they wouldn't be by my own hand. . . .

WANT MORE OF STEFAN'S DIARIES?

READ ON FOR A SNEAK PEEK OF THE ASYLUM*!*

I squeezed my eyes shut, wishing I could blot out the past and focus on the gentle swaying of the train car. My brother, Damon, was somewhere on the train, feeding on an unfortunate passenger or planning his revenge on Samuel once we arrived in London. Most likely, he was doing both. I glanced at Cora sitting next to me, a Bible still open on her lap. The cover was frayed and the pages were dotted with smudges. It had obviously been well read by someone. But there was nothing in the Bible that could help her—or any of us in this car of the damned.

In the distance, I heard footsteps marching down the aisle. My heartbeat quickened. I sat up, ready to defend myself against whoever came around the corner: Samuel, Henry, some other vampire minion I had yet to encounter.

I could feel Cora tense beside me, her eyes growing wide with fear. I reached an arm across her, as if that could protect her from a demon with a thirst for blood. A hand reached around to pull the curtain of the carriage open. I recognized the ornate lapis lazuli ring that matched my own and breathed a sigh of relief.

Damon had come back.

"Look at this!" he sputtered, waving a newspaper in front of my face.

I grabbed the paper from his hand and gazed at the headline. JACK THE RIPPER IDENTIFIED BY EYEWITNESS. Below the block letters was an illustration of Damon, a sketch done by the police, but the features were remarkably familiar. I read the caption underneath: SOCIETY MAN DISCOVERED TO BE UNHOLY KILLER. The train lurched. We were like mice on our way into a snake pit. All of London now thought Damon had been committing the Jack the Ripper murders.

"May I see that?" Cora asked, holding out her hand expectantly. But Damon ignored her.

"They could have run a better picture of me, at the very least. That illustration doesn't do me justice at all," he said sulkily as he settled on the bench next to me and crumpled the paper up into a ball. But I could see his hands were shaking with the faintest of tremors, invisible to the human eye. This wasn't the confident Damon I knew.

Next to us, Cora rifled through the papers that were lying next to our untouched breakfast trays.

"We're only a few miles outside London," I said nervously, looking at Damon. "What will we do when we get there?" After all, the quiet sanctity of the train was temporary. We were on the run, and for all we knew, we'd be found as soon as the train arrived in Paddington Station.

"Well," Damon said, throwing the wadded newspaper to the ground and stomping on it for good measure. "I've heard that the British Museum is exquisite. I haven't had a chance to see it yet."

"This is serious, Damon. They're looking for you. And once they find you . . ." I shuddered. I didn't want to think about what would happen if the Metropolitan Police found Damon.

"I know it's serious. But what am I supposed to do? Hide for eternity because I'm being framed for a crime I didn't commit? Samuel needs to pay. Besides, I'm not afraid of the police. I have a few tricks up my sleeve."

"You're in this paper, too," Cora said quietly, holding up the front page of the *London Gazette*. This had no illustration, only a headline: JACK THE RIPPER DISCOVERED, STILL ON THE LOOSE.

Damon grabbed the paper and quickly scanned it. Then he turned to me. "I look like a pauper now. I don't think anyone will recognize me," he said, as though convincing himself. Lacing his fingers together, he smoothed back his hair, then rested his head in his palms as if he were a sunbather at the beach.

I glanced at Damon. It was true: He didn't look at all like a member of London's elite. His shirt was torn and blood-spattered. His eyes were tired, and he had a shadow of a beard covering his chin. But he still looked like Damon. His hair was dark and thick, falling in a wavy line over his strong eyebrows, and his mouth was set in his usual half sneer.

Noticing me observing him, Damon arched an eyebrow. "I know you're thinking something. Why don't you just say it?"

"We shouldn't be going to London," I stated flatly. After all, Damon was a wanted man in the city. He was weak, friendless, and we had no idea how many other vampires were in London. I knew Samuel's brother, Henry, was one. We had no idea how far Samuel's reach could be. He certainly had friends in high places to frame Damon to the media.

"Not go to London?" Damon spat. "And do what? Live in the forest and wait until we're found? No. I need revenge. Aren't you concerned about your little friend, Violet?" he added, knowing exactly why I was after Samuel in the first place.

I looked at Cora, who was still desperately rifling

through the papers as though one of them contained a map with our path to safety. Her blue eyes were wide with fright, and I was impressed she'd been able to hold her head high after the events of last night. She'd been brave in the hours before sunrise, when we'd been hiding in the woods and waiting for the search party to pass, despite the fact that her sister had just been turned into a demon. Now I could only imagine the thoughts swimming in her head.

"I want to rescue Violet. I do," I said, hoping that Cora could sense my sincerity. "But we need a plan that's prudent. We don't know what we're up against."

Even as I said it, I knew Damon would never agree. When he wanted something—romance, champagne, blood—he wanted it *now*. And of course the same applied to revenge.

Out of the corner of my eye, I saw Cora set her jaw. "We have to go to London," she said in a low voice. "Violet tried to save me. I need to save her," Cora said, her voice rising on the word *save*. She folded the paper with a crisp smack and pointed at another illustration. I winced, expecting to see Damon. But instead it was a line drawing of Samuel, a profile shot with his chin held high, and his hand raised in a poised, political wave.

"Let me see that," Damon snatched the paper from Cora's grasp. "'Samuel Mortimer, the hopeful for London councillor, vows to keep the City streets safe. "I'll kill the

Ripper with my bare hands if I have to," Mortimer promises, to cheers of approval,'" Damon intoned, reading from the text. "I'd like to see him try."

I winced. Samuel *Mortimer*, derived from the French word for dead. Of course. And neither I nor Damon realized it, even as Damon was so proud of calling himself Count de Sangue. *Count of Blood*. It had probably been Samuel's first clue as to Damon's true nature.

I wondered what other clues we'd missed. I shook my head. Hadn't I fallen into Samuel's trap, too? I'd believed Damon was the Ripper.

"Promise you won't do anything until Violet's safe," Cora said. "And then, yes, kill him. Just promise that Violet won't be a pawn."

I didn't want to give Cora a promise I couldn't keep. I wasn't even confident that Damon and I could defeat Samuel, and I knew Damon wouldn't pass up any opportunity to try. I wanted to tell her to run away from all of this, as far as she could. To go to Paris, change her name, and try to forget the past. But she wouldn't. Violet was her sister, and she was bound to her. Just like I was bound to my brother. Forever.

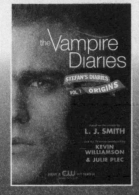 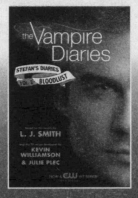 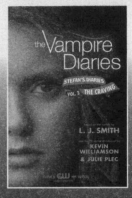